I've travelled the world twice over,
Met the famous: saints and sinners,
Poets and artists, kings and queens,
Old stars and hopeful beginners,
I've been where no-one's been before,
Learned secrets from writers and cooks
All with one library ticket
To the wonderful world of books.

© JANICE JAMES.

AFTER THOUGHTS

In this second volume of auto-biography following I WANNA TELL YOU A STORY, the Cockney entertainer tells stories of his East End childhood, of his RAF days, of his post-war showbusiness successes and friendships with fellow comedians like Frankie Howerd, Eric Sykes and Tommy Cooper, and of his world travels, particularly his American tours with the legendary Judy Garland.

MAX BYGRAVES

AFTER THOUGHTS

Complete and Unabridged

ULVERSCROFT
Leicester

First published in Great Britain in 1988 by
W. H. Allen Ltd.,
London

First Large Print Edition
published September 1990
by arrangement with
W. H. Allen & Co. Plc,
London

British Library CIP Data

Bygraves, Max
    After thoughts.—Large print ed.—
    Ulverscroft large print series: non-fiction
    1. Great Britain. Entertainments.
    I. Title
    082791.0924

    ISBN 0-7089-2279-1

Published by
F. A. Thorpe (Publishing) Ltd.
Anstey, Leicestershire
Set by Rowland Phototypesetting Ltd.
Bury St. Edmunds, Suffolk
Printed and bound in Great Britain by
T. J. Press (Padstow) Ltd., Padstow, Cornwall

For Louise, Lily, Tallulah,
Oscar, Ashley, Barnaby and
especially Michael

Preface

BLOSSOM is the name of my wife —we married when we were both nineteen; she doesn't like me idle, or making noises around her kitchen—she likes it when I am occupied. The reason, I think, the union has survived, is mostly because of the technique she uses in getting me into gear. Recently, we were packing for a world trip that, for me, was part-work, part-vacation. It was for ten weeks, I would perform fifty-three concerts, with stops in Los Angeles, Tahiti, Sydney, Perth, Tasmania, New Zealand and some names that I would like to forget, like Warnambool and Deniliquin.

As we packed our four suitcases—two each—she asked, "Are you putting any writing material in?" I asked her why I needed writing material; it would be enough performing in concert and travelling thousands of miles. She said, "I know you—you will be bored in a week if you haven't got something to fill the hours."

I argued I had nothing to write about. I wrote two books back in the mid-seventies, found it hard work and laborious. I don't type so the thousands of words required would have to be in longhand. I am not brilliant journalistically . . .

Blossom stopped me there. "You have had a most interesting life on this earth, there is much to tell—even if you don't publish it—our six grandchildren would get to know you more . . ."

I told her I had put down quite a lot of my life in the first book, *I Wanna Tell You a Story*.

She shook her head the way she did to admonish our three children when they were small. "Max—look—Jesus Christ was born in Bethlehem. After a few days, nothing was heard of him until he was in his thirties. A few years after that, he walked about telling a few stories—then the crucifixion—you have lived a lot longer than he did—look at the volumes they've written about the good Lord Jesus . . ."

I honestly don't know how she arrives at this logic. I could have filled in with a few games of golf or cruised around Sydney Harbour, but I didn't. I packed a dozen felt-tip pens and three legal pads and got very absorbed in the project Teacher had set me.

It was really written for Louise, Lily, Tallullah, Oscar, Ashley, Barnaby and Michael, but if it gives you, the reader, a few smiles—welcome—because that's what I've tried to do.

Max Bygraves
Sydney 1988

1

THE First World War had been over for four years. My father, who was named Henry but was called Harry, had been demobbed with a gratuity and a limp. *The gratuity caused the limp—he kept it in his sock.* After serving seven years with the Royal Army Service Corps, he was given £47 by the War Office; he then became a civilian. In 1919, with his brother Jim, who had lost a leg in the war, they travelled to the Derby at Epsom. My father backed three winners and left the track with almost £60—a fortune for anybody then to have in their pocket. *In those days, for sixpence it was possible to go the theatre, get a programme, a bag of nuts, ice cream and typhoid.*

On the train back to London, some "gentlemen" sharing the carriage asked them if they'd like to join in a little card game called "Find the Lady". Jim and Harry joined in and were allowed to win several times. To cut a long story, the "gentlemen" relieved them of most of their money. When Harry and Jim got off the train at Waterloo, they had roughly £4 between them. Harry had promised to marry a local girl named Lily McDonnell in a few days' time. At twenty-three, he was about to face the world with a wife, no address and thirty shillings in his pocket. *They couldn't even afford a wedding ring—it was the first time at our church anybody had ever said,"With this tap washer I thee wed".*

Luckily for them, some "rich" sod had kicked the bucket. *Couldn't call him a "poor" sod, otherwise he wouldn't have been able to afford the bucket.* Number 7, Rye Buildings, became vacant. Almost before the old boy was cold, Lily and Harry moved in on condition they paid eight shillings and fourpence a week for the rental. *Had the LCC known how many times our two lovers were going to dodge their rent collector, they would have issued them with a tent.*

Lily was a good-looking, flaxen-haired girl of eighteen when Harry said those four magic words: *"You aren't, are you?"*; later their first child was born. It was the fashion in those days to name the first son after the father. *You'd be amazed how many kids in our district were named after their fathers; there was Prudential—Provident—one lady had twins she called Legal and General.*

The first-born of our brood was Henry, who was called Harry; he was eighteen months older than me. My father, realising the army were not paying him any more money, suddenly had to decide to make a living, so he spent a long time wondering about this, *nearly a full minute*, and decided to become a professional boxer. He was quite gifted at this sport, and although he weighed only nine stone seven pounds, he was pretty useful and for his size, five feet four, immensely strong.

He had fought hundreds of bouts in the army and knew a bit about the fight game. He was still a good-looking man and had managed to keep away from the pugilistic look that so many fighters acquire. *He had a boxing friend called Basher Bailey. Basher got knocked down so often, they say he had a cauliflower bum.*

Harry Senior adored "Harry Junior".

My father was strong-willed and loved it when young Harry displayed his stubbornness; he could see himself mirrored in many ways. He could never guess how those two wills were to clash in later life, but back in the early Twenties, he would bring his cronies up to the flat to have a look at young Harry. He worshipped him and it must have been very touching to see this man with the killer instinct cuddling his first-born with a gentleness that seemed a contradiction. I think that is what made him try for me, son number two. *He didn't have to try all that hard, one wink at my mother and next day she was reaching for the maternity smock.*

Swan Lane Buildings was, and still is, situated in the heart of London's Dockland. The shape of these buildings reminds me at times of those aerial shots showing Northern Ireland cell-blocks, but not so luxurious. The River Thames flows along some twenty yards away. As a small boy, I thought the Buildings were massive, but on occasions such as "the Buildings revisited", I realised how small they really are. In these half-dozen five-storey blocks, two hundred and forty families were housed. I guess that even today I could run round the entire blocks in less than two minutes.

They were named after the Cinque ports —Winchelsea, Hythe, Rye, Sandwich, Dover and New Romney—that was the nearest us kids ever got to the seaside; in those buildings there were dozens of children and, most of us substituted the Thames for beaches at Brighton or Bournemouth. *In those days, the Thames was so polluted—if you fell in and drowned, you came out ready embalmed.*

The flat the Bygraves occupied was a one-bedroom, one-living room apartment, okay for a one-child family, two would be a squeeze, three children was nigh impossible. Little did Lily Bygraves, my mother, guess that she was going to have six children, put up her father, and that nine of us would have to live in this environment until Adolf Hitler came along to shake down the plaster and allow many of us to be evacuated. We would then discover how people outside our ghetto lived.

Harry Senior and Lily were not too badly off, not compared with other residents. He was getting a couple of fights a week and picked up ten pounds for a win, three pounds if he lost. If he was on a winning streak, that meant twenty or thirty pounds a week, and when you remember that the average weekly wage was less than three pounds at that time, my parents were affluent people.

My father's father they called the Captain; he wore a mariner's peaked cap and sang sea shanties long after he had finished with the sea. After he had sunk a couple of pints of porter, he'd get stuck into a few choruses of the most ribald ditties:

It was the good ship *Venus*
By God you should have seen us;
The figurehead was a whore in bed
And a bloke with a bloody great penis.

This was followed by tut-tuts from my Irish grandmother from Limerick, who would throw her eyes heavenwards, murmuring, "Please God forgive him."

They had six children, of whom my father was the second youngest. Grandad was constantly teasing my grandmother. Sometimes she would wax lyrical about her homeland: "Oh," she'd say. "Ireland is so beautiful—the grass is so green."

The Captain would mutter, "It bloody well should be—you're all over here walking on ours!"

It was strange how they met. She had emigrated to America with her family and finished up in Philadelphia. As a seventeen-year-old parlourmaid she worked for a German family in one of Philadelphia's large mansions. At the same time, my grandfather, who was in his mid-twenties, sailed into port on a steamship that needed repairs. During the three weeks they were in dock, the Captain met Harriet, my grandmother. He courted her and proposed to her. She accepted, then grandfather had a chat with the captain of the steamship and asked whether Harriet could come back to England with them. The captain agreed, providing that Harriet did the cooking for the crew. Several weeks later, they steamed up the Thames and disembarked just below Tower Bridge. They found a house in Abbey Street and there they spent the rest of their days. They were both twenty-five years old when they were married.

Now middle-aged, they paid occasional visits to the Buildings to see their grandchildren. He with his peaked cap at a jaunty angle, she in a wide-brimmed felt hat held in place with the longest hat pins imaginable.

As a small boy, I would sit there enthralled by the stories of their travels and the way they made ends meet. The poverty was almost Dickensian; it seemed the locals would pawn their most treasured possessions and in many cases, their most valuable assets were their false teeth. They would pledge these dentures on a Monday morning and redeem them on Friday when they got paid. *Harriet would never pawn hers until Monday afternoon because on Monday mornings she baked pies and kept the teeth for crimping the edges.*

Of course, if the teeth were not redeemed, the pawnbroker would sell them off. We had a neighbour, a Mr. Johnson, who had this permanent grin because he'd bought a secondhand pair two sizes too large. *They actually got him the sack from his steady job—he was a pallbearer at the funeral parlour.*

Into this depression, yours truly was

born. I weighed in at 10¼lb, one pound more than brother Harry. My father couldn't muster the love for me he had for Harry. *I was left on so many doorsteps, I was beginning to think I was a bottle of milk. One day, I asked my mother, "Am I a bottle of milk?" She said, "Course not —get back in the fridge."* They decided to christen me Walter William. That was shortened to Wally—an unfortunate name to be saddled with in this day and age.

When I started to put down these memoirs, I promised myself I would not be crude, but it is hard to have survived Rotherhithe without being a little indelicate, so let me tell you how it was for the family Bygraves: I am not trying to pretend we were suffering, because almost every other family on the estate was also trying to survive; our only yardstick was the folk who managed and those that did not—we were among the "did nots". For instance, some families planned to have one or two children—not ours; by the time I was ten our parents had six, my brother and me plus four girls, all with Irish Christian names: Lily, Patricia, Kathleen and Maureen. My father was a fairly strict

9

Catholic and although he practised the "rhythm method" I think he must have been tone deaf because the babies were coming in very quick succession—*If my mother missed a year, the district nurse would send her a reminder.*

The older women passed their wisdom on to the newly-weds so that if a girl wanted to terminate a pregnancy, they would give them the magic formula which was: drink a half-bottle of neat gin, then get into a hot mustard bath. *I'll never forget the girl next door to us getting married—she walked down the aisle blind drunk and yellow!*

Another way was to fall down the stairs, very hard to do if you lived on the ground floor. The joke going around among the adults in those days was, "You want to stop a pregnancy? Take six Beechams Pills last thing at night—that way you're never in bed long enough for anything to happen!" *My mother once asked the doctor what she could do to stop having children and he suggested a Dutch cap. When she told my father, he said, "If it's going to be a posh affair, I'll wear my bowler!"*

It is hard to explain that amid all this poverty lurked humour, but it was noticeable when a few of the neighbours got together for a drink or two. Mrs. Scales (Emma) had a powerful Sophie Tucker-like voice; she was a large woman with a half smile that never left her face. She reminded me of somebody who was amused by the world but was never going to let it get her down. On Saturday nights, she would stroll out of the local, the Adam and Eve, then from three hundred yards away, you'd hear the same song every week . . . "Me and my shadow—strolling down the avenue . . ." Then she would stop the singing and go in to a soliloquy; this was really talking to herself but if you cared to listen, you could. I would sit on the bottom of the steps and take in everything she said, and every week it was different.

Mrs. Scales was a widow and I believe she got a fairly good pension as her husband had been in government employ. She was always nicely dressed in a two-piece navy-blue costume and her auburn hair was always set in the same style. I liked her very much; she had a kind way of talking to you and would often give you a few coppers to spend on sweets. I remember one weekend when I was sitting listening to her, she addressed herself to me: "Young man," she said, "the day will come when you'll be old and nobody will care a sod . . . don't matter what you've done—who you've helped or what you've been . . . they won't care . . ."

Swaying unsteadily, trying to focus on my small figure sitting there, head in hands, she went on . . . "and remember this . . . you can't buy your youth when you're growing old . . . nor your life when the heartbeat has gone . . . you can't buy your way into Heaven . . . though you may possess wealth untold . . . and just like your mother, you can't buy another . . . if you had all the world and its gold."

She looked at me, her only audience, and said, "Do you understand what I'm saying?" I shook my head from side to side, there was a long silence, the half smile increased to a full one, then in a voice only a quarter as loud as the one she had been using, she said, "Well, if you don't understand what I'm saying, I might as well piss off." And she did. "Me and my shadow strolling down the avenue . . ." You could hear her until she climbed the ten flights of stairs and closed the door behind her.

What I didn't realise at the time was that Emma Scales could remember lyrics of Victorian songs from way back and make them her philsophy. I once heard her recite the verses of "She's only a bird in a gilded cage". I suppose had she had the chance she would have been some sort of orator. She was the only poet I ever knew as a small boy and I find myself thinking of her quite often.

Some faces make an indelible impression in early life. Another character that stands out in my memory was Sid Read, the local bookmaker. Sid had a pitch at the end of the street and there the local punters would hand him their bets. He had a couple of lookouts and should the old Bill patrol that neck of the woods, the spies would whistle their pre-arranged signal, Sid would scurry towards his nine shillings-a-week flat and wait until the trouble had passed. Sid was the only man in the Buildings who had a trilby hat;

13

every other man without exception wore a flat cap. On the odd times he did wear a cap, it was a vivid black and white check. He was a large man, I guess about fourteen stone, and on one occasion I saw him and my father have a stand-up fight over the outcome of a bet.

My dad had, would you believe, a sixpenny treble and all three horses won. Sid paid my father twelve shillings and sixpence. My father argued that there should have been another threepence to come; they came to blows and both of them failed to hear the runner's signal. Consequently, two uniformed policemen marched them off to Paradise Street Police Station for fighting in the street. When they appeared before Mrs. Campion, the magistrate at Tower Bridge Court, they were bound over to keep the peace. Outside the Court, they got stuck into each other again, arrested once more, and were promptly fined ten shillings each. So my father made nothing on his bet and Sid had to have hospital treatment for a fortnight. For many years after they laughed about this incident; had the policemen gone through Sid's pockets they would have found dozens of betting slips, and as he often laughed, "I'd have been sent to bleedin' Dartmoor!"

Friday night was bath-night with syrup of figs. A galvanised tin bath was put in front of the fire during the winter months and the water was poured in from saucepans that had been boiling on the"hob". It was always a case of ladies first, so my four sisters would have their bath, then my brother. I was usually last. It was like climbing into an Irish bog. *Trying to find the soap was like looking for Geoff Love down a coal mine.*

After I had dried on the same towel that had dried the five bodies before me, I was given a large spoonful of the syrup of figs. I preferred this to the castor oil that we were sometimes given on a half orange to kill the taste. The next day, there was a continual queue for the loo. My mother believed in regularity, even if it *was* only once a week.

To be fat in those days was to be prosperous, several pounds overweight and it was understood you got the excess from either eating or drinking well. There were no fatties in our family. *We couldn't even afford cutlery—we ate with our fingers—it took an hour and a half to finish a bowl of soup. If a fly landed on one of our plates, we'd grab a leg each then fight each other for the wishbone! Something we never saw was a chicken; the first time I saw a chicken lay an egg, I thought it had dropped it by mistake. I spent half an hour trying to push it back again, I'd have done it too if I hadn't broken the broom handle.*

The Buildings are situated in Rotherhithe Street, which runs alongside the Rotherhithe Tunnel. In those days, at one end of the road was the gasworks, near by was a glue factory and Fisher's Wharf unloaded some of the most vile-smelling imports imaginable. A boyhood pal of mine I met recently called it "The street of a thousand aerosols".

Up and down this street, before eight in the morning and after the five o'clock whistle in the evening, hundreds of men who worked on the wharves, or at the docks, would be scurrying home in the hope that they could get their sweat-sodden clothes off before they caught a cold. If that happened, there was no sick pay and doctors still had to be paid. On the meagre meals, that lacked vitamins, it was not easy to keep fit and in shape, consequently few men lived to a ripe old age. It was accepted that a man in his fifties, after working in the docks, would pop off with what almost everybody round that way called consumption—every ailment that killed them off was called that —the coroner didn't argue, he would write on the death certificate that So-and-So had died and that was good enough for his surviving wife to draw her widow's pension.

Some of the men lived longer, but unless a man was really tough, he didn't make it to very old age. If he did survive into the seventies or eighties, he was usually sat in the corner, with a half ounce of shag, rolling his own cigarettes, coughing to his heart's content. Old Mr. Dempsey who lived next door to us had a half ounce of Nosegay daily. With that he'd roll himself thirty cigarettes using Rizla fag papers. *One day he sneezed and got a fall of soot!*

My father now was well past his best and had to give up the boxing game; he was getting knocked down so much promoters were considering advertising on the soles of his shoes. There were many fighters younger and hungrier. So, in the early thirties he hung up his gloves and became a full-time unemployed casual dock labourer. This meant that he would have to keep his ear to the ground to find out where the big ships were docking. When he did find out, he'd get up early, run or walk very fast, to the particular wharf and then stand there with dozens of others, hoping to get picked for work. If you were a good worker and the ganger liked your face, he'd point to you, then if you had been lucky enough to be picked, you got on to the job, took your coat off and by three minutes past eight, you were working. If, on the other hand, you were not chosen, you would wander back home to kill the time until the following morning when you would try again. If there was "nothing doing", it meant getting your card stamped each day at the Labour Exchange, then, on Fridays, you'd get dole money.

My father, who had many months without work, would be paid twenty-eight shillings to survive the week. For this, there was rent and insurance, and food and drink to feed eight very hungry mouths. I still can't think how they did it. How could a family of eight be clothed and fed on less than one pound a week, even when money was worth so much more? One of the ways we were fed in the winter was from a large cauldron of Irish stew that was always simmering on the hob. It contained four penn'orth of lamb scrag end, and the rest was stewed vegetables that were bought cheaply in nearby Albion Street market late on a Saturday night. If one hung around the greengrocer's stall around 11 p.m. he would "sell off" any vegetables that looked as if they wouldn't last until Monday. There was no refrigeration in those days so a few apples and oranges with the "specks" cut out, made a passable fruit salad on Sunday. If the greengrocer liked your face, he'd throw in a banana or two. It was the same in summer with lettuce or cucumbers.

We were given cut lunches to take to school—thick slices of bread spread with Echo margarine, dipped in sugar crystals, plus a ha'penny to pay for a bottle of milk which was sucked through a straw. God help you if you threw that straw anywhere in the school playground except "the bin". Because I was tall it was thought that I was strong, so I usually landed the job of milk monitor. This meant lugging great crates of full bottles up four flights of stairs, giving them out to the pupils, collecting their ha'pennies, then giving the thirty-eight coins to the teacher, one shilling and sevenpence in all. I didn't mind this job because it gave me a chance to "trade": there were some kids that detested milk; I loved it, still do, so I'd trade two slices of bread and sugar for their bottle of milk.

When I was about ten, I got a job helping Mr. Dowsett the milkman; for this I would get two shillings a week. This entailed what I was already doing, but I did it before I went off to school, delivering the full bottles, then, for an hour at lunch-time, running up and down the stairs collecting the empties . . . *sometimes my father would creep into the flat, find my mother in the tiny kitchen and slip his arms round her waist. Without looking up, she'd say, "Two pints please,*

*milkman." This really annoyed my father
'cos it was the butcher we owed money to!*

It was expected that as soon as we were
able, we would do jobs like selling newspapers, cutting firewood or helping the
baker with his deliveries. The money
earned was put in the family kitty and that
helped my mother with the endless task of
providing.

I remember, just a couple of years ago,
I was driving along the motorway with one
of my daughters and Leslie Thomas was
on the radio plugging a book he had
written. Leslie is a fine writer and no
slouch at selling himself. It came out in
the interview that he had been a Barnado
boy and as an orphan had endured some
rough days. It took me the rest of the
journey to convince my daughter that
compared to us, Dr. Barnado's orphans
were living in the lap of luxury. I tried to
tell her that they got three good meals a
day, clothes were provided with several
changes, hair was cut regularly and they
had a bed they didn't have to share with
three or four others. Baths were provided
and all their ailments were noted by a

21

matron; furthermore, they weren't sent out to work.

Later on in life, I did quite a bit of charity work for the Barnado homes and I remember thinking to myself, "Christ—I wish we'd had it this good!" What I find hard to credit is that my father would take my brother and me for Sunday walks to Petticoat Lane; on the way we would walk through Stepney Causeway, where the Barnado Home was situated. My father who, at that time, hardly had two pennies to rub together, would drop a couple of coins in the box to help the orphanage. I must remember to ask Leslie Thomas for a free copy of his next book, tell him that without the subsidy of the Bygraves family, he might have been a failure.

Going to bed as kids was a pain in the neck, well a bit lower really. Before my parents purchased a bed to go in the living room, the children were bunged into one bed slightly larger than a single size, all except the youngest, Maureen, who was still being breast-fed. So, brother Harry, myself, Lily, Patricia and Kath had to share, we slept head to toe . . . *I've never been able to look a tin of sardines in the face since!*

My sister Kath had a bed-wetting problem, we really couldn't do much about it. When she went to sleep and my brother and I were still awake, this warm feeling would start to spread as she began to leak. Harry's comment would be, "Oh no! the tide's coming in again!"

Lily was the tomboy of the family—everything my brother and I did, she had to emulate—kicking a tin can, playing cricket or trying to out-swim us at the public baths. One winter, Harry and I tried to write our names in the snow by doing a pee—Lily had to try and copy us. *She pulled a hamstring muscle when she tried to dot the i.*

Patricia was the forager of the family; she used to run errands for a wealthy household and they gave her unwanted clothes to bring home. *Once she brought me a pair of shoes, no toes—no heels—no soles—I wore them for a week before I found out they were "spats".* She once brought home a pair of trousers for brother Harry; my mother spent three hours trying to let them down before she realised they were "plus fours". You can't imagine how many times I wished I was an orphan in the security of Dr. Barnado's.

The chances of meeting a rich person were as remote as meeting someone who had actually won a *Reader's Digest* draw. The men we associated with riches were the "tallymen"; they usually wore collars with ties, matching suits and horn-rimmed spectacles. They also carried thick black books with customers' names and addresses; they were a sort of mobile Marks & Spencer's. There were many housing estates and these were their quarries; they treated this terrain as "never-never land" and they (the tallymen) were the "good fairies". Going from door to door, they would sell goods on instalments. A woman could buy a new outdoor coat for sixpence a week over forty weeks —and most of them did—but the only trouble was, because of the high birth rate, for twenty of those weeks, she couldn't button the damn thing up. When the baby was eventually delivered, the woman's stomach was fine—it was the coat that had "stretch marks".

And how those poor ladies had to live

on "pledged" goods. Round in St. Mary's, Church Street, was A. J. Cohen Ltd., pawnbrokers. After the goods were bought from the tallymen, the buyers would use them for a few days, dust them off, then take them round to Cohen's and pawn them; he would pay the women a quarter of their value. If the women could afford it they would be redeemed on the Friday night. Cohen would take anything—suits, shoes, sheets, pillow-cases, teeth!

I remember one Easter as a small boy, lying in the luxury of some new sheets just bought on hire purchase. It was the smell of fresh linen that has stayed with me always. On the Monday, they were stripped from the beds, taken to the local wash-house in Gomm Road, brought home, dried in the square with the iron posts for putting lines up, then gathered in, pressed with an iron that had to be continually heated on the gas stove, afterwards wrapped up neatly and taken to Cohen's. For all this effort, he would allow two shillings. If they were redeemed, an extra ten per cent had to be paid as interest by the pawner. If the goods were not redeemed, they "ran out", and Cohen sold them.

I only spent two nights in those crispy white sweet-smelling sheets—when Ma pawned them and we never saw them again. It was back to the blanket with Dad's army greatcoat over us. *If we complained to Dad that we were hot and couldn't sleep, he'd say, "Lie on the edge of the bed—you'll soon drop off!"*

With money so tight, you had to get the maximum value from everything you bought. My dad thought the greatest value of the day was the *News Chronicle*. First, you read it . . . then you used one sheet as a table cloth . . . another sheet folded up would cover the holes in your shoes . . . one more sheet would light the fire . . . the rest cut into squares would be hung in the lavatory. So, for a penny you got the news . . . a tablecloth . . . a shoe repair, a firelighter . . . and a toilet roll.

My father was always trying to make his fortune; he had a good brain for mechanical devices, the world was really getting into gadgetry and he was most interested. One day, he fished an old cork lifebelt out of the Thames; it was the type used in those pre-war movies, the sort that extras sang "Abide with me" in, the kind the hero handed a young lady with the line, "Here love, you need it more than me." Then the young lady, sitting safely in the lifebelt, watches our hero go under and mouths the words, "Goodbye, Charles," the tears flow—the music swells—roll credits.

I thought this lifebelt hung in our passageway because the flat was so damp some day one of us would need it. Harry, at one time, was thinking of wearing it when we shared the bed with Kath the bed-wetter. I was surprised to come home from school one day to find my father prising a circle of cork out of the front of the life-belt with a kitchen knife. Into the hole he had made, he was putting a bicycle lamp with a new Ever Ready battery. He made a neat job of sealing it with sticking plaster. The idea he had in mind was for people lost at sea to switch the torch on and so be seen from long distances for rescuing. It was a novel idea and he figured that if somebody like Lloyd's of London saw it, they might reward him with a few quid—at this time, he was constantly thinking of anything that might make life easier and take him out of that degrading dole queue.

On a Saturday morning, I walked with him to the City, he with the lifebelt in brown paper tucked under his arm, I walking beside him trying to keep up. Across Tower Bridge, up Leadenhall Street to Lloyd's. A large commissionaire at the door inquired if he could help; my father asked if he could see somebody to show his invention to. The commissionaire asked what sort of invention it was and Dad told him. A look came over his face and he shook his head slowly. "I doubt if you could get to see anybody without an appointment," he said. "Why don't you pack it up, send it registered post with a diagram to our Mr. Hudson at this address?"

Dad never got round to doing it; for one thing the registered post was too much for his empty pocket.

Almost a year later, he read in the paper of an identical idea that had been approved. Till the day he died, he wondered whether the commissionaire had nicked his invention.

Apart from the two rooms we lived in,

28

there was a short passageway in from the street, a scullery on one side, a loo on the other; past the loo was a coal cupboard and above that a gas meter. Consequently, my mother had to do both the cooking and the washing in the small scullery, which couldn't have measured more than 4 by 6 ft. There was a permanent smell of boiled cabbage and stewing socks and the way Mum cooked, it wasn't easy to tell the difference until you ate a spoonful—the socks tasted better. *At mealtimes, we'd play "musical dumplings"—it worked like this—my mother would put a dumpling on a plate . . . my dad would start playing his harmonica . . . then we'd pass the dumpling round from one to the other . . . then, whoever had it in their mouth when the music stopped was allowed to swallow it!*

Also, in the scullery, Dad would shave. Each morning I could hear his open razor being stropped against the leather. The song he sang as he shaved was "The Sunshine of Your Smile". He had a light tenor voice that was not unattractive and as we all filed in one at a time to wash our

29

hands and faces before going to school, he would good-naturedly dab the shaving-brush on the tip of our noses. It is hard to imagine that there was quite a huge amount of love and warmth circulating in those couple of rooms; it was a rare day we weren't all laughing at something or other, but the poverty got no better, neither did the living conditions—in fact they got worse. My parents were praying for the day my brother and I would be leaving school to go out to work to earn our keep.

When I had finished my newspaper round, the newsagent would give me a copy of the *Evening News* which I took home. My father would read it, then find a pencil to give me the clues in the children's crossword; he would get angry with me if I came up with the wrong answer. My mother would sit there nursing the youngest and if I could not answer, she would mouth the word behind my father's back; my father would say, "Right—a capital city of India—five letters?" If Ma could see I was stuck, silently she'd spell out D-E-L-H-I without my father getting wise. Why I remember this particular incident was because my mother was furiously pointing at her stomach, hoping I would rhyme Delhi with belly. I got a clip round the ear when I said, "Er—stomach?"

After serving four years in France, my father had a good idea of the language, so each evening he'd give us a lesson in French, and woe betide us if we could not remember the previous evening's lesson. With his forefinger, he'd prod me hard in the stomach between each word: "How—(prod)—do (prod)—you (prod) expect (prod) to (prod) grow up (prod) sensible (prod) if you (prod) don't bother (prod) to learn (prod—prod—prod!)

Things were getting beyond a joke in the flat. My brother was now fifteen, I was coming up for fourteen. Lily was twelve and had started to grow bosoms—at one time she was putting bread poultices on them, she thought they were blind boils! Our sex education had ben nil, my father was as shy about this sort of thing as we were. I recall once walking with my dad through Southwark Park and saw two dogs locked together. He tried to walk away and divert my attention to a game of football being played, but I insisted, "Dad, what are those dogs doing?" He cleared his throat several times and, seeing he had to give some sort of answer, he said, "Well, the one at the back has got a bad leg and the one in front is giving him a piggy-back to the infirmary." I just said, "Oh", then turned and watched the football match. I read recently that Noël Coward was credited with this, but my dad said it first.

You can guess how overcrowded we were and on top of all this our grandfather, who had been poorly, moved in—there was nobody to look after him at his digs in Kings Cross so we had to make room for him at number seven Rye Buildings. I am talking about my mother's father, Walter McDonnell, a true gentleman: considerate, kind, articulate and very handsome. He was in his late fifties, walked erect, had the most beautiful white hair and dark eyes that turned the local ladies on, they almost curtsied as they passed him in the street, murmuring, "Good morning, Mr. McDonnell."

Grandad was a tradesman, a leather currier, and he worked for Connolly's, who still supply the leather for Rolls-

Royce cars. He worked hard and looked after my mother with a couple of pounds' supplement periodically. If he visited Rye Buildings and saw the soles of our shoes hanging off, or the seat of our trousers missing, he'd "tut—tut", fish in his pocket for a ten bob note and say to my mother, "Lil, take them up to Tower Bridge Road and get them some shoes." Next morning, we'd all board the 68 tram, my ma would shop around and probably get four pairs of shoes for the ten shillings.

It stood to reason that she would look after Grandad, because apart from genuinely caring for him, she didn't want this source of revenue to dry up. As I said, Grandad McDonnell was a gentleman and was thought of as a dandy. His survival kit was a simple one. About once a month, he bought a large bottle of eau de cologne from the local chemist; he would then add several spoonfuls of olive oil, and when this was well shaken together he'd use it for almost everything personal. If there was any sign of dandruff, he would use it to take the dryness out of his scalp; he would rub it into his hands and feet should they show any signs of dry skin; after shaving—long before after-shave lotion became fashionable—he'd pat it into his cheeks, then after bathing he'd rub himself down with it. There was a freshness about him that not many shared in our part of the world and it was all down to the eau de cologne and olive oil lotion.

The "mixture", as I got to call it, accompanies me on all journeys around the world and it cures most of the ailments I have mentioned. This, besides Grandad's advice always to "dry between the toes" causes great amusement among my own children, who think I am a bit eccentric, but I notice that now they are married with children of their own I often hear the same advice being handed out, also there is always a large bottle of "the mixture" in the bathroom cabinets.

Several years later, Grandad died—it was the first death we had ever known in the family. I had joined the RAF by then and because I was with a squadron involved with the Battle of Britain, I was refused leave to get home for the funeral. I remember lying in my bunk and crying myself to sleep at his passing. I loved the man, and every memory is of the fondest.

2

AT last I am fourteen and my parents are ready for the good life because it means that my brother and I are at work and hopefully supplementing the family budget. It is 1936 and things have become a little easier, the depression has eased slightly. Very few have realised that Great Britain is shaping up for a war with Germany and the extra jobs have come from preparing for it.

My father was finding more ships to unload at the docks, my brother was working for a haulage contractor known as Thos. Allen; he had a pair of horses that he loved to drive at the gallop, then enter the road to our Buildings like Ben Hur on his chariot.

I started work for an advertising agency called W. S. Crawford; their offices were at 233 High Holborn, next door but one to the Holborn Empire. I started as a messenger boy and it was my duty to run copy to all parts of London. Most of the deliveries were in Fleet Street and three or four times a day I would have to go to newspapers like the *Daily Express, Daily Telegraph, The Times*—almost every London and provincial newspaper, to collect what is known as "proof" copies.

There was no uniform, we provided our own shoe leather, we worked from nine in the morning until six in the evening, Saturdays from nine a.m. till one p.m. and for this I was paid fifteen shillings a week. It was compulsory to wear a tie with a clean collar each day, our hair had to be parted and brillianteened, there was also an inspection of hands and fingernails, all this to lug newspapers and the lead printing blocks used in those days up and down Fleet Street.

There was a rise of five shillings at the end of each year and one could hope to get into the £6 a week bracket in seven or eight years, providing you worked hard and were always on time. This is what I accepted and my hope that one day I might rise to the rank of dispatch manager, like Mr. Pearce or Mr. Wrench, who had been messenger boys themselves and now ran the dispatch department.

Secretly, what I liked about the job was that once or sometimes twice a week, I could pay for admission to the Holborn Empire, a music-hall type of theatre that had all the élite of the variety acts performing there. It was only one minute away from Crawford's. How did I get the money for the admission? I "fiddled". If I was given the full fare to deliver a package to say, Gillettes out on the Great West Road, I would travel to Piccadilly Circus, then buy a cheap day return; this was a saving of eightpence. Sometimes, if a load of proofs or blocks was too heavy to carry, we would be allowed "taxi money" with a threepenny tip for the driver. I figured I could do with it more than the driver, so, risking a hernia, I would board a bus with the full load and "stick" the fare. A few "fiddles" like this and it wasn't hard to make an extra five bob a week. That was enough for more admissions to the theatre or cinema or, as I found myself at that age, gravitating towards the dance halls. Also from these perks, I was able to buy a bicycle from Gamages on hire purchase for half-a-crown a week. This also saved eightpence a day fare money from

Rotherhithe Tunnel to High Holborn, so from the fifteen shillings a week wages, I was able to "give up" twelve shillings a week towards my keep; this meant, after insurance stamp and superannuation was stopped, I was left with two bob a week pocket money—I don't know how I would have managed if I hadn't been at the "hi—diddle—diddle".

Puberty for me was purgatory. One day at the swimming-pool I was drying off. I raised my arms and noticed hairs under my armpits; my first thought was, "Oh my God—my stuffing is coming out." When I removed my swimming trunks and looked down, I noticed the appearance of whiskers around my crotch. When I told my father about it, he said, "That's God punishing you for misdeeds—he's turning you into a coconut!" It really was a waste of time confiding in him.

I never got round to telling him that on mixed bathing days, with girls the same age parading in their swimsuits, I had to keep diving in the pool to take the swelling down. Also, whenever I gave a girl a ride on my bicycle crossbar, it made me breathe heavily. I remember Annie Johnson saying to me, "Every time I go for a ride on your crossbar, you make my glasses steam up!"

Added to all this, I was an altar boy. At Mass, I would have to hold the plate in front of the recipient's mouth whilst the priest popped the host in. Some of those young girls with their mouths wide open filled me with thoughts that no young man should have had in church. Further, I could never bring myself to tell Father Leahy of these terrible fantasies when I went into the confessional box—if I had, my penance would have been trebled.

Luckily, I was interested in sport and got a chance to put these horny thoughts out of my mind, then there was the music hall and the cinema, which was okay if a gangster movie or a comedy was showing, but the feeling would return if Jean Harlow or some similar siren was on screen showing lots of leg—thank goodness it was dark in there so one could keep one's thoughts private.

We never saw graffiti; I remember in one of my television shows I stood in front of a wall with graffiti scrawled that said,

"Keep Britain tidy—export Patrick Moore"; another read, "Save a hamster—stop Scargill wearing a wig"! It was exaggerated of course, but there are few places in the world nowadays that don't have beautiful buildings desecrated by aerosol-happy fanatics.

When I was young, you never saw graffiti, for three good reasons . . . a third of us couldn't write . . . a third couldn't read . . . and the other third couldn't do either. Consequently, if we went to the "flicks" to see the silent movies, to understand the plot, we learned to lip-read. It's a habit you don't seem to lose. Even today when a player misses an open goal on "Match of the Day" . . . I can tell every word he says.

The local cinema was a flea-pit in Jamaica Road called The Storks, a little run-down place. *They couldn't even afford an usherette—they'd trained a cat to walk backwards down the aisle with one eye closed.*

Most of us had been going there since an early age to see the serials with stars like Tom Mix and Gene Autry. It was a way for our parents to get us out of the house on a Saturday morning. My first memory of Flash Gordon was at the Storks. *Many years later, I met the actor that played Flash Gordon in Hollywood— he was seventy-six—just called himself Gordon!*

The great thing about the films we saw was their innocence, there was never anything suggestive at the Saturday morning flicks. *In fact, the only full frontal we ever saw involved Rin Tin Tin and a tree.*

The Hays Office, plus the British Censor, made sure we were never corrupted in any way. For example, if an actor and actress were involved in a bedroom scene they could never be seen in bed together . . . the man had to keep one foot on the floor at all times. *A bit like playing snooker without a cue!*

What a dump the old Storks was. Sometimes we would leap out of our seats and do an impersonation of James Cagney, we'd say things like, "You dirty rat you!" The only difference was we were talking to *real* rats. Unlike the youngsters now, we never experienced hype or rock 'n' roll, there was nobody that had the energy of

Bruce Springsteen or Mick Jagger. The nearest we got to excitement of that kind was a high kick from Jessie Matthews, or seeing a big band concert, or having the Salvation Army playing outside your window on a Sunday evening. Believe me . . . it's not easy trying to jitterbug to "Jesus wants me for a sunbeam".

There seemed to be a lot less crime too. It was perfectly safe for a woman to walk the streets alone at night . . . many of them did . . . and made a good living at it. Another reason it was safe to walk the streets was that in our district you hardly ever saw a car, everything was delivered by horse and cart, so the air was free from car fumes . . . you had to be careful where you trod though. Us kids use to collect it in a bucket then sell it to owners of flats that had window-boxes; they would pay us a penny a bucket. One Sunday, I made a small fortune: it was the week the Bertram Mills Circus was appearing at the New Cross Empire . . . I was so grateful to the elephants.

A few years before my fourteenth birthday, I had tasted fame. As a soloist,

I had sung at Westminster Cathedral with our school choir. We had won a trophy that made us the best in south London; my solo of "Jesu Joy of Man's Desiring" was reckoned to have swayed the judging panel; consequently, if a family was having a party celebration of some sort, there would be a knock on our door with an invitation for my mother, but, be sure to bring Wally. By then, I had got myself a small repertoire of songs—mind you, a person found fame at a party if he or she could remember the lyrics of a full chorus.

There was very little pop music on the wireless—even if you were lucky enough to own one. A few neighbours had gramophones, but most of the recordings were of brass bands or Dame Nellie Melba—at least the gramophone owners I knew had these. So, to hear a young lad with an angelic voice giving out with songs like "It's My Mother's Birthday Today" or "Buddy, Can You Spare a Dime" not only got rapturous applause from the half-sozzled audience, it also earned me pennies for my efforts. Sometimes I would leave a party with as much as a shilling. Slowly, although I wasn't planning it that way, I leaned more and more towards show business.

My father had taught me a song he had sung in the First World War, so with a battered khaki cap that he had actually worn during his years in France, and with a broom as a rifle borrowed from the lady of the house, I would perform, "Why Did I Join the Army". I think this song must have been composed by a soldier in the trenches because although I have tried to trace the writer or publisher, the search has proved fruitless. I have written other verses for my one-man show but the chorus I gave out with as a twelve year old went . . .

Why why why did I join the army?
What am I doing in the Fusiliers?
Why did I have to sign . . . along the
    dotted line?
What am I doing here in Armentiers?
I must have been out of my mind, I
    must be barmy
Kitchener's got a lot to answer for
Up to my neck in mud and grit
Everywhere the smell of it

Oh how I'm longing for Blighty's
   shore . . .

Of course, the audience knew the "mud
and grit" line had been cleaned up by my
father; this caused great merriment to the
dockers and tough stevedores who usually
made up the audience. I was now getting
used to entertaining. Far from being shy
about performing, I found myself looking
for parties to show off at. I was also being
asked to shindigs outside the Buildings so
by the time I left school, I had built a
quiet reputation as an entertainer and even
if I didn't get a "collection" at all of them,
invariably I was invited to have some food,
and as a growing lad I could eat enough
to compensate for wages.

The job at Crawford's took me to all
parts of London. A delivery I detested
most was to Price's the candlemakers at
Battersea. They usually advertised in the
glossy magazines like *Country Life* or
Vanity Fair—to take a dozen proof copies
on the tram from Kingsway to York Road
in Battersea was heavy going with a long,
uninteresting ride to boot. It was on one

of these trips that I was introduced to homosexuality.

As lads, we were aware of what we called "nancy boys"; they were harmless and actually joined in the fun of "sending up". We knew of two who used Rotherhithe Station for "trolling". It was amusing to us when with rouged cheeks, marcel-waved hair and darkened lashes, they would mince to the station ticket office and buy a return to Leicester Square, where, no doubt, they were treated to gin and tonics by "friends up West". What we were not aware of, and nobody prepared us for, was the homosexual who was "butch" and looked like a replica of Primo Canera, the heavyweight champion of that time. My first experience of this was on a 38 tram going out to Price's at Battersea one summer morning. I always went "on top" for the long journey and on this particular day, the upper deck was practically deserted. This meant at least thirty empty seats so I was most surprised when a man, who I guess must have been in his forties, came and sat down beside me. He was well dressed in a dark grey suit, stiff white collar and highly polished brown shoes. I moved over to give him room; he smiled and began to fill his pipe from a pouch. "This doesn't bother you, does it?" I shook me head, "Er—no", I said. He asked me if I smoked. I told him I didn't, he said he thought I played a lot of sport—I answered I did, we talked about some London football teams for a while, then he asked me what position I played on the football pitch, I told him I usually played defence. His eyes lit up: "I thought so— I thought you'd be something like that— you've got the legs for it." With that, he put his hand on my thigh on the pretence of feeling my muscle.

Something told me all was not right, but I felt it would be rude to do anything like ask him to keep his hands to himself—not only that, he was a well-built bugger who looked as if he would give me a clout if I raised any objection. He began to rub his hand up and down my thigh as he spoke of living alone in Lambeth. He told me that he did all his own cooking and that he could take me back there and show me some magazines that were filled with pictures I had never seen before. He began to breathe like I did when I got Annie Johnson on the crossbar.

Oh Christ, I thought, how do I get away from this man? I had already told him I was going to Price's in York Road, that meant at least another twenty minutes away, so I couldn't pretend it was my stop coming up. He now started to write his address on a piece of paper with instructions on how to get there. He reached in his pocket, then gave me a sixpence to cover the fare to his flat from Rotherhithe, and said he would expect me the following evening at seven o'clock.

The conductor came up top checking tickets, saw the two of us seated in the same seat, looked around at the empty deck and, obviously suspicious, said to me, "You all right, son?"

Before I could answer, the man with the pipe said, "Yes—we're just talking football—he plays—don't you!"

I stammered, "Yes." I have been around the world more than twenty times but that fifteen minutes to Battersea felt like the longest journey ever. I thought it would never end.

That same evening, my father was

reading the *Evening News*, my mother was knitting. I told him about the man on the tram, that he had given me sixpence to visit his flat. I saw a look go from him to Ma, and both their brows were furrowed.

"Send it back to him," he said.

"How?" I asked.

"Like this." Dad then found an envelope, wrapped the sixpence in tissue paper, addressed the envelope, then made me take it to the post-box and drop it in without a stamp on. When I returned, I thought, at last I am going to get some sex instruction. I said, "Dad, why didn't you want me to go to that man's address?" He turned his newspaper over to the front page. "Here's why," he blurted. The thick banner headlines screamed BRIGHTON TRUNK MURDER. Some maniac in Brighton had carved a body up, stuffed it in a trunk and left it at Victoria Station. An attendant became aware of a "foul smell" and reported it. When opened, the trunk contained the torso of some unknown which was now the biggest story of the year.

"Because what's happened there—could happen to you," shouted my father.

"Going home with people is taking your life in your hands—next time anybody approaches you with this request, say, 'Can I bring my father?'" Still no counselling, still no reason to be wary of strangers, poor old Dad, he just couldn't get round to putting it in words. It didn't stop the warmth I was getting around the loins whenever I thought of girls.

Annie Johnson was a real turn-on, apart from her glasses, she had to wear braces, not on her teeth, but to keep her knickers up. She came to see one of my shows a few years back and told me she'd had nine children (she said the elastic in her braces had perished).

At about thirteen, Annie had developed a beautiful body and the gang of boys I went around with would drool when she wore her tight sweater. Bras were unthought of in those days and as she jumped up and down in the middle of a skipping rope, it was just too much for us to watch. One late evening during the summer, half a dozen of us were discussing films. We were on some steps beside the Thames, the tide was out and there was just the sound of water lapping quietly among the moored barges, the moon shone on the river, the silhouette of Tower Bridge in the distance gave the scene what lady novelists sometimes call "romantic surroundings". Annie was arguing that the best kisser among the male film stars was Clark Gable. "Yeah," I said to be cute, "he kisses just like me!" Annie took her glasses off and said "Show me!"

Our lips met to kiss the only way we knew, with lips closed and eyes open, slowly her lips parted, then she pushed her tongue into my mouth and began to wiggle it about. *I didn't know it was supposed to excite me—I thought she was after my chewing gum!*

It was my first kiss and it made me rather eager to try it again. Frannie Miller was another young lady ready to have a go at anything once—once a night that is. *During the war, she went out with so many American servicemen, she was known as "Yankee Doodle Bandy!"*

At least Frannie was responsible for putting me right about a few things. Up till that year, I was convinced that women got pregnant, then after nine months the baby entered the world through the lady's navel. She also told me what those sausage-like balloons with the teats on that filled the Thames in those days were for. It was Frannie that first told me the joke about the young boy who walked into the chemist's shop and said to the lady behind the counter—"Three contraceptives, please miss!" The lady said, "Don't you 'miss' me!" The boy said, "All right—make it four!"

Oh dear, I was so very naïve compared to modern-day children—I don't know whether it's a good or bad thing—we were so innocent, but at the same time the world unravelled slowly, and it seemed more exciting. As a youngster, I cannot remember being bored for one single minute and although there are many luxuries by today's standards, almost everything worth having then had to be achieved. If you have not lived in those days, you cannot appreciate how difficult it was to become the owner of a three-quid bicycle. I was surprised when I bought a bicycle recently how little the machine had changed since I was a youngster. I am not talking about the racing—daredevil—chopper—twelve-speed type of two-wheeler. I mean the good old steady "get you there with no problem" bike. The frame is the same, the wheels and chain are practically the same, the saddle bag, the lamp-holder and brake principle are roughly identical to those I used and travelled hundreds of miles on as a teenager.

In those days, once you got your parents to sign a form as a guarantor, you could go to Gamages in Holborn or James Grose in Euston Road and for 5s. down, plus 2s.6d. every week, you could purchase a bike for roughly £3. 10s.6d. I had to give a solemn promise to my folks that I would be responsible for the repayments. How I loved that bicycle. You had to know a thing or two about "Old Blue", know how to judge the pressure in the tyres; too little air would almost make you bite your tongue off as you rode the cobblestones from Tower Bridge down to Rotherhithe Tunnel where I lived. On the other hand, if you inflated just a wee bit too much, the inner tube would explode like a firecracker and unnerve you for the next three days.

There was an oblong tin that held the

puncture outfit; this was filled with different-sized patches, a tube of glue that had an alluring smell, I was so hooked on this smell I could have been one of the original glue-sniffers. There were valve rubbers, plus a sort of talcum powder that stopped the tube sticking to the inside of the tyre. You also kept a few more valves for emergencies.

In the saddle-bag was a lock and key with a cable that deterred "nicking", because no matter what your grandmother tells you about people being more honest in those days, there were just as many "tea-leafs" that would take it away if they saw it unattended for too long.

We were just as short-tempered with the Police Force then as a lot of people are today. I remember once being stopped for not having lights after lighting-up time. For this, I had to lose half a day's work and appear at Tower Bridge Police Station, where the magistrate, Mrs. Campion, fined me five shillings. I recall my dad saying, "Pity the police can't find better things to do, such as stopping agitators like Oswald Mosley . . ." I nodded my head in agreement. I didn't mention that if I knocked somebody down and maimed them because they didn't see me without a light, I might have finished up in Wormwood Scrubs. The Police were only doing their duty. But my father had a very quick left hand, so it was much wiser to nod agreement.

The gang I "biked" with had different thrill areas. One was to go to the top of Shooters Hill, then come down at thirty miles an hour and hope the brakes would hold at the cross roads if the traffic lights at the bottom were red—a memory that makes me shudder nowadays.

Another trick that now brings me out in cold sweat was to overtake a horse-drawn cart along the main road. It meant cutting the middle tram line at an acute angle. If you didn't make it, the wheel went down the opening, over the handlebars you'd go, the spokes would be ruined and if there happened to be a number 68 tram coming up behind, you could be pushed sixty or seventy yards before the driver could stop. Luckily, there was Guy's Hospital at one end of the road and St. Olave's at the other, so an ambulance was usually very prompt in arriving. Now I've got a couple of Rolls-Royces in the garage, but coming down Shooters Hill in one of those just isn't the same as on "Old Blue". *I still have a bicycle, but it doesn't have a crossbar—I find that as I get older, it's harder to get your leg over!*

3

WORKING for Crawford's gave me an insight to the world of advertising. It became evident that a logo could say in a word what would normally take reams of copy to convey. For example the Milk Marketing Board had a poster that used a sky-blue and navy-blue dab of paint with MILK in white superimposed and it said it all.

Worthington, the beer, used, "He's twice the man . . ." across an athlete in action.

Heinz, the baked bean people, was recognised by number 57. Incidentally, many years later, I was invited to lunch by Cecil Beaton at his home in Barbados. He was a charming man and sat me next to Mrs. Heinz, an Irish lady named Kath, who told me the story of how the 57 trademark originated. The Heinz family were Germans who had emigrated to America at the turn of the century; they prepared pickles and soups which they sold to the neighbours. So popular did they become that the house next door to them in Philadelphia was purchased to cope with the orders. They built a successful business in the States and decided to expand overseas.

Mr. Heinz travelled to London and bought some land for a factory out at Harlesden. One day, he was travelling down to Brighton and noticed a huge hoarding advertising footwear. The styles of the shoes included lace-ups, button-ups and elastic-sided boots; there were nine different styles altogether and the logo for this was a 9 in a circle. On the train from Victoria, Mr. Heinz began to add up the different varieties of soup he was marketing; it totalled fifty-seven, and although the number has varied over the years, the firm still keep the Heinz 57 logo to this very day.

I have never employed a press agent or publicity service during my career but advertising made me aware of how important it was to have a catchphrase. I have had many, including, "A good idea son", "Bighead", "I wanna tell you a story", "Big Money!", "Dollar lolly", "SingalongaMax", which has been permutated to "CongalongaMax", "Laugha longaMax". My last television series was titled *LingalongaMax*. The wonderful thing about these catchphrases is that with so many impressionists on television these days, they actually do the job of advertising you. Years ago the main place to advertise was on hoardings that were eye-catching. I once wrote a piece about those ads and I called it "Bill Stickers RIP":

D'ye remember those placards and
   posters
They posted on hoardings up high
Remember the man with the bucket
   and paste
And a ladder that reached to the sky?

He'd take out a poster some twelve
   feet by six
Then cover the back part with glue
And there it would stay—for a year
   and a day
As the world down below stopped to
   view.

He pasted up posters for Bovril
R. White's advertised ginger beer

Wincarnis was wine that made you feel fine
Especially if you were queer.

There was young Denis Compton for Brylcreem
And glacier mints made by Fox;
And one I remember said, "Take Beechams Pills—
They're worth a guinea a box!"

Jacob's Cream Crackers—Libby's Tinned Milk
And biscuits made by Peek Freans;
They advertised Eno's to get rid of wind
Right next to an ad for Baked Beans.

"Horlicks" is one that stays in my mind
"Horlicks"—will stop night starvation.
And little square chocolates called Ex Lax
For people that had constipation.

One ad that made the unemployed smile

They thought it such a big joke
"For only six hundred—own a Rolls-
    Royce!"
Most of the poor sods were broke.

There were posters for weekends in
    Paris
And seaside resorts down in Kent.
There was one that simply said—
    Durex
I was too young to know what that
    meant.

But now they've all vanished—Bill
    Stickers is dead,
His ladders and paste you don't see
He's gone, like the man with the pole
    that lit lamps
And for this you can thank ITV.

It doesn't come up to John Betjeman's
standard, but it makes me remember the
prime sites that More O'Ferrall sold to
advertisers in those days. I recollect an
incident when I was waiting for my hair
to be cut at Ivan's in Jermyn Street. The
door opened and a quiet white-haired man
sat down beside me. Out of the corner of

my eye, I could see it was the great Charlie Chaplin, or Charles as he liked to be called. He was in England to promote a movie he had directed, *Countess in Hong Kong*, which starred Marlon Brando and Sophia Loren. He seemed a friendly sort. I nodded to him, smiled and said what a pleasure—a genuine pleasure it was, to meet him. In the middle of our conversation, the barber walked up and said, "Ready now, Mr. Bygraves".

Mr. Chaplin suddenly became animated. "Bygraves? Max Bygraves—you are in a show at the London Palladium."

I nodded. "How did you know I was at the Palladium?" I curiously asked.

He replied, "I saw it on half a dozen hoardings driving in from Heathrow."

Which goes to prove that, doesn't matter what sort of success you've had in life, if you are a pro you never stop searching the billboards to see if your star is still twinkling.

Back to the Buildings; I was now fifteen and the only direction in life was to work hard at Crawford's, hope to get promotion, have a regular job, find a local girl to court and marry, then after that, a family and an LCC flat with not too many children. Three nights a week I went to evening classes and learned shoe repairing, which saved my folks large amounts, for our boots and shoes took an enormous bashing and were constantly needing repair. I also did woodwork and found that extra shelves made lots more room in the flat, something that had never entered Dad's head.

The other nights I went to a music hall, either the Holborn Empire or the New Cross Empire. I had won a go-as-you-please competition, being rewarded with £25 first prize, so although I was going to the show to enjoy myself, I was also watching the technique of the performers. There was one artiste, named Albert Whelan, who had the strangest act you ever saw. He would enter in tails and top hat with white gloves on; as he removed the gloves he whistled a song; when they were off, he would drop them into his top hat, then tell a couple of stories. After the patter, the band would strike up again, he would replace the top hat, start whistling once more, put the gloves back on and exit. *He had a very large following—mostly dogs!*

Never being able to afford the expensive seats, I had to go up to the gallery, and that made the performers seem very small indeed. *The first time I saw Wee Georgie Wood I thought I'd gone blind.*

But they could project their voices—if they didn't, it wasn't unusual to hear a voice near by shout, "Speak up, we can't 'ear yer!" Sound systems were not what they are today. Sometimes the microphones would oscillate and the helpless performer would look off stage, step away from the centre to finish their act without the aid of the mike. I have had a few fail on me over the years. I usually thank somebody up there for the ability to work without the microphone though I don't like to because with radio, records and television, audiences are microphonically receptive and we just don't sound the same without electronic help.

One man who did not need any help from the sound department was Max Miller. He was a first-class comedian who rarely went above Birmingham to appear; his audience was London or Brighton, and so secure was he in his ability, he stipulated to managements that unless he could catch the eleven o'clock train to Brighton after the show, he didn't want the engagement, and they usually juggled the bill around so that he could leave the theatre in plenty of time to make his train.

I got to know Max fairly well; I worked on several variety bills with him and we did a season together at the Palladium. When Eamonn Andrews surprised me with his red book for *This Is Your Life*, Max came on and when Eamonn asked him if he had any advice to pass on to this young fellow (me) with the same name, Max said, "Yes—always be on time— always work hard on your material and never—never—tell a blue joke!" Coming from the most ribald performer of the day, he walked off to the loudest applause of the night.

That was in 1963, when Eamonn Andrews presented *This Is Your Life* for the BBC. When he passed away recently, I was reminded of the time when he, Tommy Cooper and I were having a drink after one of the shows. Eamonn said to Tommy and me, "Do you know—we three are the most impersonated men in Great Britain today—if anything happens to us, half the impressionists in the country won't have an act." Now with Tommy and Eamonn gone, one can't help thinking, "Who's next?" I hope I complete this book before I'm called up.

The last thing we thought about in those teenaged days was leaving this earth. I lived every minute of every hour of every day—when my head touched the pillow— and though we were down to three in a bed—all male—I slept like a log.

On Saturday nights, our gang of half a dozen would "ponce" ourselves up to go to the Palais de Danse, or the sixpenny hop as it was better known. This large dance hall at the top of Deptford High Street had a live band, there was a dance floor that could accommodate five hundred dancers and a spinning crystal ball that was lit by a spotlight. The romance this brought to couples meeting for the first time is legendary. *All it brought to me was the advantage of that soap—the one that prevented BO!*

Come Saturday night and I'd put half a tin of Vaseline on my hair, part it to gleam like the poster of Richard Green, who advertised Brylcreem—that was a good hair cream but not as good as Vaseline— after using Vaseline the remainder of the tin could be used for cuts and burns, for rough skin and for rubbing in your leather football boots. Brylcreem, on the other hand, was twice as dear and was no good for chapped lips.

The first question we asked a girl partner was, "Come 'ere often?" As soon as you got her chatting, the follow-up question was, "Where do you live?" If she lived the opposite way to the 47 bus route going to Rotherhithe, you'd give her a miss. If by chance she was heading your way, you'd risk paying her tuppence fare to "see her home" as an investment.

It was all very innocent; you would probably get a kiss and a cuddle on the doorstep before her father's voice boomed out, "What bleedin' time d'ye call this?" The door would open and her old man would say to her, "Get inside!" Then turning to me, he'd say, "You—piss off!"

By now, the last bus had gone and you'd have to walk the rest of the way home to Rotherhithe Tunnel where your mates would all be standing round the coffee stall eating hot meat pies and supping mugs of tea. As soon as you were seen, they'd ask, "Get anything?" It depended on whether you made a story up about a raver you'd been with or you played the part of a gentleman and kept your secrets to yourself. I always played the part of the gentleman—mainly because I never "got anything".

My father frowned on me going with girls. *I think he was saving me for a part in* The Sound of Music. At the same time I think he was relieved that I wasn't gong out with blokes like the one I had met on the Battersea tram. My mother had visions of me studying for the priesthood and became quite concerned when, as a teenager, I began to miss Mass on a Sunday morning—this was considered "mortal sin" and as I became less enchanted about going to confession on a Saturday night, all she could think of was the gang and the awful influences I was going around with; she told me she often said prayers for me. I was keener on learning how to quickstep and foxtrot than studying to work "the one-day week!" A joke I regretted when I got a clip round the ear from my father for being disrespectful.

At the same time as I was growing to be a seventeen-year-old, my brother Harry was almost into manhood. He was tall and strong, he spent a lot of time at the gymnasium, had grown almost nine inches taller than my father and slowly, he began to challenge the "old man". At first they would spar up but Harry fancied his chances and would try to outwit Dad. If he did get one over, the old man would get angry and what started out as a friendly "shape up" usually became fisti-cuffs with a capital F.

My mother would try in vain to break them up but they were obsessed with beating the hell out of each other. Eventually, my father lost control and threw a right hook that broke Harry's jaw. For several weeks, young Harry had to go to work and walk the streets with a frame on his head as support. My mother made us younger ones promise we would never tell any outsiders how it happened and to pretend that Harry had fallen and broken his jaw. There was no society that was too interested in child abuse in those days, if there had been, I'm sure my father would have gone away for several years, especially as he had been a professional fighter. Nothing came of it, and my dad, filled with remorse for his temper, was repentant and became much closer to Harry.

Dad was keen to have both Harry and me follow him into the boxing world. To make sure that neither of us would back out, he would fit us with boxing gloves, then before he shouted "time", he'd tie the shoelaces of both our left shoes together; that way we were rooted to the spot and we would have to duck and weave to stay out of trouble.

Many years later, when Harry became a successful publican and I became the allegedly highest-paid performer in Great Britain, he once said, "I thought I was going to have two welter-weight champions—instead, I've got one who serves drunks in a pub and another who goes on stage making a bloody fool of himself."

It was now getting to the time where Harry and I would have to think of fighting quite seriously. It was 1939, the

70

dark clouds over the English Channel were looking quite ominous, Adolf Hitler was occupying countries all over Europe, Neville Chamberlain, the Prime Minister, wasn't doing too much to stop him and we were both coming towards call-up age.

4

THE first inkling we got that war was imminent was the issue of gas-masks to everybody—babies included. These awful-looking things were to be put over the face in case of a gas attack. Some people were so nervous of this happening, they wore them throughout the day. The streets were blacked out; it wasn't unusual to bump into old maids with hopeful looks on their faces. They practised with the sirens, a terrible wail that we eventually got used to, but at first it was a terrifying noise. Mr. Chamberlain came back from Munich, then on British Gaumont News, he assured the country that after a conference with Adolf Hitler, there would be peace in Europe. We all went to our beds that night relieved that we could get on with our lives, no worries about gas attacks or running into air-raid shelters.

A year after that announcement, on 3 September 1939 at 11 a.m., the Prime

Minister told us we were at war with Germany. The black-out started the same day and so did the jokes . . .

Air Raid Warden (to house not too well blacked out): "Oi, there's a chink at the window!"

Voice from house: "That's nothing—there's a jerry under the bed!"

The armed forces had theirs too: Soldier (on guard in black-out): "Halt—who goes there?"

Girl's voice: "You don't expect me to say 'friend' after the way you behaved last night."

It was the general feeling that it would all be over in six months so we weren't all that worried. It affected me in a way because Crawford's had to close down. Newspapers, for economy, had been cut down to a broadsheet, consequently, there was no space to advertise. Almost the entire staff, apart from us young messengers, were of call-up age, and they were recruited into different branches of the armed forces. *One fellow in the copy department was called for a medical and he pretended he had one leg shorter than the other. They passed him A 1; he asked why and they told him, "Don't worry, the ground ain't level where you are going!"*

I was still in my seventeenth year, too young for call-up, but Harry couldn't wait to get into uniform; almost on day one he joined the Royal Engineers and after some heavy training down in Kent, he was sent to France with the British Expeditionary Force. *I remember being the first one off the boat—running up the beach shouting, "Come on lads, don't be scared—follow me!" I was court-martialled for that—we were still in Dover!*

Still a civilian, I went to a small village in Kent called Paddock Wood and got a temporary job picking hops on a farm owned by Whitbreads'; it lasted for three weeks, then I returned to London. The most plentiful work was in the building trade. I got a job with a firm called F.G. Minter; they were building the air-raid shelters for the workers at Crosse and Blackwell's soup factory in Bermondsey.

My job was as a carpenter's apprentice; this was a way of not paying you too much money because you were supposed to be learning the trade in their time. The carpentry I did was negligible. I spent most of the time sweeping up, making the tea and sharpening chisels for the carpenters who had already served their seven-year apprenticeship. Still, the money was comparatively good. I was being paid twice as much as I had been getting at Crawford's, which was handy because we had lost one of the breadwinners when Harry joined up. Dad was now in regular work as most of the young dockers and stevedores had been drafted. He vowed that after seven years as a soldier in the First World War, four in the trenches, they would never get him in uniform again; he was still in his early forties. The government then came out with a scheme that dock workers could be sent to different parts of the British Isles, depending where the shipping had been directed. Dad was sent to Liverpool—Glasgow—Wales—he hated Wales, he was a friendly man but he couldn't hit it off with Welshmen.

I once overheard him tell one of his mates a story which I wasn't supposed to hear, because, apart from a few "bloodies", he wasn't into profanity—come to think of it he was, by today's standards, a very good honest clean-living sort of chap. The story was about the docker from London who mentioned to a friend that he couldn't get on with the Welsh—they were too cliquey and would never invite you to join in their conversation. The friend said, "Next time you go into a pub, raise your glass and say, 'Yacky da!' They'll talk to you then."

So the next time he went to Cardiff, he did as the friend advised. He raised his glass to a chap standing next to him, smiled and said, "Yacky da!" The chap looked straight at him and in a Cockney accent said, "Piss off, yer Welsh bastard!"

I was itching to join up, but I was still under eighteen and would not be eligible until my next birthday, which was still a long way off. The one joy of my life was a carpenter named Albert who belonged to a small concert party that went round to different air-raid shelters giving concerts. The party consisted of Albert, who did a red-nosed comedy bit, two lady singers, an accordion player and a baritone. They worked out little cross-talk routines and usually finished with all of them taking part in "If I was not upon the stage" for the finale.

It was all pretty corny stuff but the audiences, who had nothing else to do except look at each other, adored it. It was all for free, and they travelled everywhere by public transport. The accordion played popular choruses and the audience joined in loud and long. Albert heard me sing at work and found I could do impressions. He talked me into joining the company and before I finished work, he'd tell me at which air-raid shelter we were appearing that night. I would have to find my own way there with the help of a torch in the black-out, then find my way back to my own air-raid shelter, which was a dugout in the square of Swan Lane Buildings.

It was long hours: I was usually up at 7 a.m. to go to work and rarely got to bed before midnight. At this particular time, there were a few siren false alarms, but things were pretty quiet considering there was a war on. Then it happened. Early in 1940, the German Luftwaffe started to bomb London and the Home Counties. We were an easy target because on moon-lit nights, the bend in the river at Rotherhithe could be seen quite clearly from the air and all the bomb-aimers had to do was drop a load at random and they were almost sure of hitting a vulnerable spot. Oh Christ, how those bombs came down—I have never been so terrified and helpless. All we could do was cringe in the shelter and hope they'd miss us.

So many times I have walked home at night after appearing with the concert party shouting out loudly, "Oh God, don't let me die!" It was nerve-racking—*almost as bad as a first house on a Monday night at the Glasgow Empire!* Strange thing was, it didn't deter me from going out with the gang, we were all amateurs and so keen to please. One of my strongest impressions was of a star named Arthur Tracy, who billed himself as the Street Singer. His big song hit was "Marta"—I had a trilby hat in the prop basket that I put on and did my impersonation of him; it got good applause and I learned to save it for my finish. I would also do ten minutes of Max Miller's act, which I knew off by heart, then join the company for the finale. In all, we did about forty-five minutes. The Cockneys down the shelters would give us tea and sandwiches, which might sound meagre but it came from their rations. If the raids were really bad they'd tell us not to go home in such danger, they would then make a bed up for us in a bunk and, fully clothed, we'd lie there till the morning hoping the Dornier bombers had returned to Germany. *"Come on gal—the sirens have gone!" She shouts, "Hang on! I can't find my false teeth." He shouts, "Never mind your teeth—it's bombs they're dropping—not meat pies!"*

I was put to work on bomb damage; if a house had been badly hit but not destroyed, it was our job to make it live-able in. We battened black felt to the windows; it kept the light out and also kept the rooms warm enough for occu-pation. I would have to climb on to the roofs to replace slates that had vanished through bomb blast. It was precarious work but if it wasn't done, the poor tenants had rain coming through their ceil-ings. Very few of them complained though, the strongest words I ever heard came from an old man who said, "When this bleedin' lot is over, I'll never buy another bleedin' German sausage!"

My three youngest sisters, with thou-sands of other London children, had been evacuated to a "safe" area, so bloody safe, I can't remember where it was. With only my mother and sister Lily at home, the flat seemed quite empty. Harry was in the army, Dad up in Liverpool and the three youngest now evacuees. *When I woke up in bed one morning and found myself alone, I thought I was dead.*

Mum had got a full-time job working for Gordon's Gin as a packer. In a way it was war work because we still had to keep our exports going to pay for it all. Lily had got a job packing gas-masks. With the three of us arriving home from work at once, having dinner was about the only time we met. Mum and Lily would wait for the siren, then hurry down the shelter, I'd go off to entertain at some other shelter —we'd see each other for a few seconds at breakfast, then it was off to work again.

5

ONE afternoon, I was working on the roof of a house in Deptford; the sirens had gone but I decided to go on working. The drone of the bombers got nearer, and out of one eye I kept watch. Suddenly, I couldn't believe my eyes, the air was black with enemy aircraft, Spitfire fighters and ack-ack fire. As I watched, I heard the swish of a bomb hurtling earthwards. It exploded no more than a hundred yards away, the roof lifted like a trampoline and I found myself slithering down towards the guttering with nothing to stop my descent. Luckily, it was only a two-storey house and as I slid to the ground below, my fall was broken by a privet hedge, and apart from a few scratches I was all right. It was then and there I decided to join up, and that same evening I boarded a bus to the Yorkshire Grey pub at Eltham and enlisted—two months before my eighteenth birthday.

The medical officer passed me A 1, and

three weeks later I was informed by post that I was to report to RAF Cardington for entry into the Royal Air Force as an Aircraftman Second Class, number 1212094. I assumed I would be back in civvies after a few months—little did I suspect the RAF would be my lifestyle for the next five years.

My entry into the RAF was a bit of a mess up: my brother, who had joined the Royal Engineers and gone to France, had to leave in a hurry via Dunkirk. Without reporting back to his unit at Maidstone, he came home, and from exhaustion, he slept for three days and nights. The evacuation had been a military success according to Churchill, and the "little ships" that carried thousands of troops back to safety was a triumph; but fellows like my brother had suffered badly, up to their shoulders in water, trying to get aboard anything that would take them. Many of them lost everything they possessed, but what made them such a sorrowful sight was their loss of dignity.

When he had time to assess it all from his bed at Rye Buildings, Harry made up his mind not to go through another

Dunkirk as a soldier in the Royal Engineers. Without a word to anybody, he "lifted" my identity card and birth certificate, then re-enlisted in the RAF in my name. In the meantime, a letter arrived from the War Office to my mother telling her they could not account for Henry Bygraves, but any further news would be sent to her when the dead and missing from Dunkirk had been ascertained. They never did.

So when I joined, there were two Walter William Bygraves, with same birth date and same parents, and the only way you could tell us apart was we had different numbers. *My father once said to me, "Wouldn't it be funny if you died and they buried him!"*

My one worry was that the war would be over before I was called, but about sixteen days after my medical, the papers arrived. I was told to report with only a toothbrush and comb to the Yorkshire Grey at Eltham. All equipment, like uniform, knife, fork and spoon, would be provided by HM Government. Up till now, I hadn't told anybody about my enlistment, although my sister Lily had a suspicion. When I had learned the song, "Why, Why did I join the army" as a kid, my father had taught me some drill movements like "One—pause—two—pause", and so on. One day, engrossed in these exercises, I did an about-turn, there Lily stood watching me.

"What's all this in aid of?" she asked. I put down the broom I was using as a rifle, then told her I had been to the attestation centre and it would only be a short time before my papers came. She was now sixteen, a worldly young lady. "You know Mum will be upset if you do go—there are no men around the house now that Dad is sent all over the country and Harry is back in the Services—she depends on you to look after all of us—you don't have to go.

When the papers arrived, it was one of the hardest decisions I ever had to make. I had been out on a binge the night before with some pals. It was a farewell party and my head was splitting from drinking rum —I was a non-drinker but was assured I would come to no harm, this by a pal who had joined the Navy as a stoker and was on his first leave. I couldn't think of how to put it to my mother, who had no idea

I was going. I took the coward's way out and left a note with some money in, on the mantel-piece.

I was told afterwards that when she read it, she burst into tears and said, "What's he doing with the RAF—he can't drive an aeroplane—he can't even ride a bike!"

We arrived at Cardington, in the county of Bedfordshire. I had the toothbrush, a razor with a new packet of three-hole blades—I still hadn't had my first shave —and twelve shillings. With about thirty other fellows, we were told to remove all civilian clothing, pack it and address it to our homes; the issue of uniforms followed. In a few hours, I was a uniformed member of Her Majesty's Forces AC 11 BYGRAVES (ACH. G/D) which stood for Aircraft Hand General Duties. At the medical, I had failed on eyesight, so hopes of aircrew training were out. I was offered the trade of a Fitter A/F (Air Frames). I would be taught this trade, but first I was to learn "square bashing", this meant drill —drill—drill at a place called Bridgnorth up in Shropshire. *You must have heard of*

Bridgnorth—they had a streetwalker there —she was fifty-three and still a virgin!

A young fellow from Greenock in Scotland and I were the youngest in the squad. Jimmy Cairns and I still hadn't had our eighteenth birthdays and we became inseparable. Jimmy had adenoids trouble and was continually sniffing. When our drill-sergeant, "Jock" Ewan, was briefing us on hand grenades, Jimmy would continually sniff—sniff—sniff. *"Have you got a handkerchief, Cairns?" Jimmy would sniff again. "Yes sergeant, but I don't lend it to strangers!"*

Jimmy was sent to the cookhouse to clean the dirty tins, and for laughing, Bygraves had to go with him. Jimmy was about five feet six with a red nose from continually wiping it. He spoke in a thick Scottish accent which almost nobody understood, especially me. I had lived only among Londoners and these "foreign" accents from all parts of Britain spoken by the men I had just met were new sounds to my ears. Consequently, these chaps were named after their home towns, Geordie, Taffy, Jock, Paddy, Scouse. I had been dubbed "Max", because of an impromptu act at a NAAFI free-for-all—I did my impression of Max Miller—it was to stick. *I sometimes wonder what I would have been called had I been impersonating Bette Davis.*

"Yorkie", who came from somewhere on the Yorkshire moors, would tell tall stories of farmers and nurserymen who hailed from his part of the world. "I once saw a lad get a bottle of whisky and drink it down in one go."

I ventured the line, "Was it neat?"

Yorkie, waiting for the feed, said, "Nay —it were middle of day!" Christ, he dined out on that story for the next twenty years.

Ben Slennet, another Londoner, was the smoothest operator I had met up till then. He was the "old man" of the squad, he was thirty-five, nearly twice my age. I thought he was very old and should never have been in uniform; he was a conscript constantly working on trying to get back in civvies, or, as we termed it, "trying to work his ticket". He was excused marching, excused PT and did not have to go to lectures. Most of his time was spent as hut orderly; this entailed cleaning the stove, bringing in the coal and "bumpering" the floor with wax polish. The whole chore took no more than forty minutes, but somehow Ben could make it last until evening. Then, we'd all come back from marches or rifle practice and flop on the beds exhausted while Ben moaned about how thoughtless we all were for messing up his polished lino. It must have been lonely for Ben spending the day by himself, but after a chat to the sergeant, he was allotted an assistant—me. He taught me to be a malingerer. "Never have the place looking spick and span," he'd say, ". . . always leave some coal or a tin of wax polish in the middle of the room so that if an officer comes in, you always have something to do."

Ben was a London wide boy and appointed himself my manager—a real Bilko. The first job he got me was at a meeting of the Buffaloes; the Royal Ancient Order of Buffaloes was comprised of gentlemen who met regularly to "further friendship and goodwill amongst men". Anyway, that's what Ben told me; he also mentioned that our fee for the evening's entertainment would be £1— that was equivalent to three weeks' pay from the RAF. Ben had chatted up the orderly officer for passes out of camp, to help the war effort, he told him. He had suggested that Bygraves would perform for the Buffs and the collection made after would go to the Red Cross and so help the wounded. The officer signed the passes, Ben and I got transport to the village and around nine o'clock, I did my party piece.

The Buffaloes were delighted; not only did they pay me the pound they'd promised, they also gave me a bottle of French champagne. Ben took 50 per cent of the fee, then on the way back to camp, he opened the champagne, which we drank between us walking up the blacked-out lanes. Even though it was warm champagne, I liked the taste. The nearest I had ever got to a glass of bubbly was Eno's Fruit Salts. I liked it then—I dislike it now.

Under Ben's management, I was booked for cabaret spots in the sergeants' and officers' messes. There was no pay for these "gigs" but we ate and drank well on it; furthermore, they got us out of many guard duties. Ben would find out where the local hospitals were, then with a few musicians, and one or two acts like myself, we would give a concert in the wards to cheer up the patients. Very few of the patients had ailments that had anything to do with the war, but they got our entertainment, whether they liked it or not.

The drummer with the trio was Ray Ellington, a massive, weight-lifting, good-natured man of West Indian descent. As I did my jokes, he punctuated them with a roll on the side drum; if I got a big laugh, he would hit the cymbals. If a joke "laid an egg", I'd get a dull sound from his foot pedal; it was a style that caught on and many comics still use the same approach today.

Ray sprang to prominence with the *Goon Show* that starred Peter Sellers, Spike Milligan and Michael Bentine; his singing style was so different it was instantly recognisable. When Ray died last year I could hardly believe it, he was so well preserved, I thought he was indestructible. When I saw his son Lance, a talented, handsome young fellow, on a television show recently, I could see that a lot of Ray's polish had rubbed off on him.

If he doesn't make it in a big way—there ain't no justice.

Ben was hustling my amateur talent everywhere. If he got a forty-eight-hour pass to London, he would go into local pubs that had "live" entertainment and sing my praises to the licensee. It wasn't long before we both fiddled weekend leave and spent it "earning" down at the London pubs. Sometimes I would "double" two pubs in a night, getting thirty bob in each, all this with sirens going, warning people to take cover; very few did. As the bombs and ack-ack guns got louder, the pianist and drummer did their best to drown the noise. One night I was giving out with "When the Lights Go On Again All Over the World . . ." Suddenly, without warning, a land-mine went off about three hundred yards away. The lights went out, the microphone went dead, the deathly hush in the pub was broken by a man's Cockney voice finishing the song, "There'll be Time for Things Like Wedding-Rings and Church Bells Will Chime" . . . as he sang another Cockney accent cut in with

"Ooh, hark—Vera Lynn's paying us a visit!"

By now, the war was getting serious and urgent, the drilling was over and many of us were posted to train for the trades we had chosen. I was posted to RAF Locking near Weston-super-Mare. This was where fitters and instrument repairers were trained. I said farewell to Ben Slennet, and we kept in touch for twenty years. After the war, Ben managed a pub in Chelsea; whenever I appeared at the Chelsea Palace Theatre I would go in to see him. He would tell his customers that he was my first manager. Ben died a few years ago but his memory is rubber-stamped.

The course at Weston-super-Mare would be for three months' training; most of the time we filed down pieces of metal, then measured them with a micrometer to within a thousandth of an inch. I never really found out why, for all the years I serviced aircraft I could never remember using a micrometer or filing a piece of metal, nor did I ever see any other mechanic do so.

"Go to the stores and bring me an oxometer."

"What's an oxometer, sergeant?"

"It's an instrument for measuring bullshit."

Roll on drum. "Thank you Ray."

It was at Weston-super-Mare that I got to know Reg and Irene Winstone. They kept a home that was open house for members of the forces. Rene, as we called her, had three daughters of school age; she would lay on tea and cakes for anybody who cared to call. She organised musical evenings and it was here I got a chance to practise. One of the airmen who dropped in regularly was Bill Davis, now known as William Davis of BBC fame. Bill could make a piano talk and where I had been singing songs in the only keys that the pianist could play, Bill was capable of transposing. All of a sudden, I was making quite pleasant sounds, I was vocalising in keys that were comfortable for me—a whole new world had opened. There were lots of free evenings at Locking and many opportunities to appear in camp concerts and charity shows in the town of Weston. I had no fear, I'd go ahead and "do a turn" at the drop of a hat. With the help of Bill Davis and the encouragement of Rene Winstone, I was putting an act together that had shape and built to a climax. I still keep in touch with Rene and her husband Reg—I have much to thank them for. I left Locking as a fully trained mechanic with an extra two shillings a fortnight for completing the course.

Posted to Hornchurch in Essex—right in the Battle of Britain front line, I joined 611 Squadron from Liverpool, the only Londoner among a whole battalion of "scousers"—all of them talked like Cilla Black. About this time, my sister Lily had added a year to her age and joined up in the WAAF. So now, the only one in the real front line was my poor old mum. The younger ones had been evacuated, three of us were in the RAF and the "old man" was every week in a different town. Almost every night London was being bombed unmercifully by Hitler's Luftwaffe. I remember one night coming home on a twenty-four-hour pass and finding Mum "tipsy" on gin—I'd never seen her in that state before. I couldn't make her pull herself together and got quite angry when she wouldn't sober up. Then I got angry with myself for feeling that way. On the train back to camp I realised that it was the only way the poor devils could blot out the raids, the bombs, the wrecked homes. There she was alone and she was frightened, and I was too bloody selfish to recognise it. I've hated myself ever since for not being more understanding—*Never mind Mum— I'll make it up to you—one day I'll be wealthy and you won't have to work any more! One of these days, I'll take you shopping at Harrods—'course that was when Harrods was still part of the Commonwealth.*

It had not occurred to me that I had lived through the most colourful decade of the century, or that I was a tiny part of it. Newspapers and magazines were always printing pictures of Noël Coward—Lilian Braithwaite, the ex-king who had abdicated—(Christ, what a bit of luck we didn't finish up with him as monarch). The 1930s had seen the élite at Henley, the débutantes and the London Pride crowd, who tried very hard to associate with the workers.

At the cinema, British actors from

middle-class backgrounds tried to emulate the Cockney. It is now pitiful to hear their attempts, but at the time we thought they were wonderful. Of course, every movie was made with the hope of an American release, so that the accents were geared for USA audiences to understand. Even good old Tommy Trinder, the Cockney comedian, seemed to go all posh for his speech delivery—catch an old film of Tommy's on television and you'll hear him sing in those plummy tones that Noël Coward used—he sounds more Noël than Noël.

Many years later, when I was appearing in *Doh Ray Me* at the Prince of Wales Theatre in the West End, Noël Coward came backstage to my dressing room, put out his hand and said, "Wotcher mate!". I was most disappointed, I was hoping he'd use the "Don't put your daughter on the stage Mrs. Worthington" accent. Actually, I got the feeling he was trying to convince me that the theatre world was all a bloody game and that we were all bloody lucky to be making a living from it.

So, with the passing of the airships, Lindbergh's solo Atlantic flight, Oswald Mosley and so many milestones of the Thirties gone, we were entering the Forties. The country was in a sorry state, we could ill afford a war, but we had gone into it singing songs that quickly became hits and just as quickly fell by the wayside, songs like "We're Gonna Hang Out the Washing on the Siegfried Line", and another one, "Who Do You Think You're Kidding Mr. Hitler." We became aware that Mr. Adolf wasn't kidding—he was winning the war —he meant business.

RAF Hornchurch was practically at the mouth of the Thames; we needed Spitfires to scramble at a minute's notice. For this the whole squadron was on "stand-by" twenty-four hours each day—there was no time for sodding about—not with squadrons of German bombers on their way to raze London to the ground. Meals were brought to the dispersal hut, then from early dawn until dusk the "on duty" men would sit by aeroplanes at the ready. As soon as the panic bell went, strap in one of the pilots, give his windscreen an extra wipe, push the starter button as soon as he gave the signal for "Contact!" Then it was

97

chocks away, as the machine took off into the blue. I would wonder if the planes and the young pilots would return—many times they did not. It was among all this chaos that I met Blossom the WAAF.

As early as five in the morning, this pretty WAAF came pedalling past the dispersal post on her issue bicycle, making her way to the cookhouse. So regular, that almost every able-bodied man in the squadron would stand at the edge of the perimeter "wolf whistling". She would answer by ringing her bell and laughing at the attention. She wore hardly any make-up, her big blue eyes were crinkled from smiling, her figure made sounds come from us like men drowning.

I was one of the admirers who toed the line admiring this teenage beauty. The men had nicknamed her "Blossom" because of her bright natural colouring. *I was still very naïve about girls—the nearest I'd had to a sexual experience was in a sick bay when a blanket bath I was having got out of hand—it came as a big surprise to me because I'd only gone to visit a friend.*

I'd had a girlfriend for a time in Rotherhithe. She was named Addie and she had this habit of sucking my neck. After an evening with her, my Adam's apple looked like a vampire's teething ring. Just before I joined up, she did something that took all the magic out of our relationship—she became a vegetarian.

But now I was nineteen and behaving "like a sheep on turnips". So full of energy, so physically fit and so frustrated . . . if I had followed my mother's ambition to become a priest, I'd have been unfrocked there and then. Oh, those thoughts that passed through my head as Blossom pedalled past, knees up high. Some mornings, I'd lie down on the grass pretending to be tired so as I could get a different angle on this girl who was making my heart swell—among other things.

By now, the autumn was fast disappearing—soon the snows came. This gave us great relief from the daylight raids; the countryside covered in white made it difficult for the bombers to find targets, so sorties were fewer, and life for 611 Squadron became more peaceful for a while. Sure enough, on Daily Routine Orders, there were requests for amateurs who could sing, dance, recite or entertain. If you felt equipped to "have a go" it meant reporting to the Entertainments Officer, which I did, not because I felt I was all that good but because there might be a faint hope of getting out of some of the dreadful guard duty and fatigues we were constantly being allotted. Unless you've stood on an aerodrome in blizzard conditions, with a 303 rifle over your shoulder (no bullets), thanking God for the Red Cross ladies who had knitted your balaclava, you wouldn't appreciate how the warmth of a concert hall was preferred. Any devious means were valid and I couldn't wait to put my name down.

The station band was a quintet made up of musicians who, in civvy street, had been personnel of top-name bands like Ambrose, Harry Roy and Joe Loss. They were the cream of the music industry. At different times, I had been accompanied by stalwarts like Norrie Paramor, Tiny Winters, Sydney Torch and many more sidemen who made up the top orchestras of the time, a luxury I had never dreamed

'Hello, Sailor!' – in Twentieth Century Fox's *Bobbikins.*

It wasn't easy making a living in the early 1950s!

Donald Pleasance cuts up rough in *Spare The Rod.*

A couple of swells. On stage at the Palace, New York –
Judy Garland is the shorter one.

With daughters Maxine and Christine –
they *still* suck their thumbs!

Above – Anthony played Charley Moon as a boy
in *Charley Moon* – he didn't need make-up.
Below – With Michael Medwin in *Charley Moon* –
he won the part from Peter Sellers.

Above – Arriving in Cape Town, lots of white people and media coverage. *Below* – The Luxurama theatre in Cape Town, the only white minstrel – but no press.

Above – You haven't lived if you haven't had a ton of horsemeat tread on your toes. *Below* – After the first year at the Victoria Palace – a day off for good behaviour.

The Variety Club Show Business Personality of 1973.
'It's nice to get an award – look what it did for the
Duke of Edinburgh!'

of in Swan Lane Buildings. They were obliging chaps, also experiencing the boredom of playing the same old routines, so a new face was most welcome. Many of them went out of their way to help make what I attempted seem that little bit more polished. If a key was too difficult it was transposed to suit the range I sang in; they were so professional and assured, to them it was as simple as shelling peas.

One morning following a concert the night before, I was struck dumb by the gorgeous WAAF Blossom, who came up to me in the mess hall with a request for the words of a song I had vocalised. The song was "If I Had My Way", a big hit by Bing Crosby about that period. "Of course," I stammered, "I'll be delighted." She smiled this lovely smile, then turned and walked away with her plate of rissoles and two veg held high so as not to spill the gravy. *I couldn't help thinking that if we ever played musical dumplings, she could have my share any time.*

I scribbled the words out, put them in my tunic pocket and hoped I would see her soon. It was another week before I bumped into her again, and during that time she had added two stripes to her uniform so she was now Corporal Murray. Funny how the higher rank of corporal made me, an AC 11, feel so inferior.

"I wrote the words of that song out for you, corporal," I blurted.

"Words? What words?" I pushed them into her hand, she thanked me, then carried on talking to another airman by the name of Cliff Michelmore (yes, that one). There I stood, nineteen years of age—a failure!

Not too long after this, another concert. As I walked on to the stage, I saw Blossom sitting in the front row. Cliff was nowhere in sight, Blossom was with a companion WAAF we called "Blondie". The song I had chosen to sing was a current hit for Perry Como. Without taking my eyes off her, I stood in the spotlight, then directed every lyric in her direction . . . "You came —I was alone—I should have known— you were temptation" . . . she was interested. I went for the big finish, ". . . I'm just a slave, only a slave to you— temptation—I'm your slave. . . !"

Without warning, the microphone went dead—the Tannoy came on, a voice boomed, "All personnel report to units immediately—all personnel report to units immediately . . ." No bloody applause— just the noise of five hundred men and women scampering from the concert hall, like a scene from MASH, as the siren wailed another warning. *I brought up my children never to use the word "hate", a word I think should be deleted from the dictionary, but at that moment I hated that bloody Adolf Hitler.*

It wasn't until a few days later, when I was talking to Blondie in the NAAFI canteen, that she mentioned her friend Blossom. "She's taken a real fancy to you." I almost choked on my Tizer. "Me?" I asked. She nodded, she had to be kidding. "Yes, you—if you asked her for a date, she'd faint—she talks of nothing else." There were more than fifteen hundred men on that aerodrome and only thirty WAAFs. Blondie had to be joking, because any WAAF could have the choice of dozens of eager males. I tried to be nonchalant, but as they say—it's hard to be humble . . . It must have been another week later, I was travelling back to camp by tube on the Upminster Line. It was late evening and as the doors of the train opened I saw a girl in uniform step into the carriage. It was Blossom. I stood up and offered her my seat, the train lurched and we fell against each other. Wow! Ten thousand volts went through me.

"Do you mind if I walk you back to your billet?" I asked. Her billet was the other side of the camp, which made it a two or three-mile walk back to the quarters where I slept. It was a freezing cold night, both of us were buttoned up in greatcoats. After we had gone through the main guard-room, I took her arm, she snuggled up close, and even in that freezing atmosphere it felt like the Sahara.

I shook hands with her at the door—no kiss—no funny stuff, then walked back in the Siberian weather to Elm Park—I was in love. *My family, who lived on the second floor of the Buildings, guessed I was in love when they kept seeing my feet go past the window.*

We started courting, if you can call courting sneaking a kiss in some air-raid shelter that smelled of carbolic, or being lucky enough to get in the back row of the stalls of the Havana Cinema in Romford.

Our one wish was that we could both be off duty at the same time because, by now, we were deeply in love. Then a bombshell—she was elevated to the rank of sergeant. Not only did she earn a lot more than my AC II pay, she had three stripes up. It was embarrassing to walk out with her and hear cries of "Crawler" from the erks that made up 611 Squadron. But we survived, I proposed to her and with hardly any money, very few prospects and no home, we became man and wife at Romford on 12 September 1942—we were both nineteen.

Our good friends, the Winstones, at Weston-super-Mare, gave us a room for a seven-day-leave honeymoon, which we spent sitting on the beach during the day, looking at miles of rolled-up barbed-wire, put there to stop any German invasion. The nights looked after themselves.

I couldn't have been happier. Back at camp, I thought how lucky I was to have fallen on my feet. A loving and caring wife, a joint pay account. I was earning on "gigs" here and there, all we needed now was the war to finish and get on with living. The ecstasy lasted just over a week: the squadron was posted to Drem in

Scotland and Blossom remained at Hornchurch.

Drem was a God-forsaken spot, in the middle of nowhere. There was little to do as it was supposed to be a rest period for the squadrons which had been taking part in the Battle of Britain. There was little chance of leave, as I had just had seven days to get married, phones were almost non-existent for people like us and letters took an eternity. Also, they were censored. I once wrote and asked Blossom to give my love to her sister in Dagenham and the word Dagenham was blue-pencilled by the censor. To make Blossom smile, once I wrote a letter which I censored myself, I wrote Darling, then I scribbled a long page of rubbish that I put a blue pencil through so that when she received the letter, it just read "Darling . . .", then a whole page of writing blue-pencilled. At the bottom, I put "Your loving husband, Max". When she received it, she wrote back to say that I mustn't be so free with my thoughts because the censor had cut the whole of my letter out! I could never convince her that it was a joke.

Eventually, after almost three months, I

got another seven days' leave. I travelled down from Scotland to a smiling Blossom, who met me at the station with the words, "Guess what?" I said I didn't know what —she took my hand, then pressed it to her tummy—I noticed the belt of her uniform had slipped a couple of notches. "We're going to have a baby." She was deliriously happy, "Aren't we lucky!"

I didn't say a lot because I thought, "Christ, what's lucky about a baby being born in a war zone with parents that haven't got a home, etc., etc . . ." It was the wrong time to mention it because I think at that moment, it was one of the happiest days of her life. She told me her discharge from the WAAF was imminent. "But I'll get a job," she enthused. Her sister Evelyn at Dagenham had a spare room and Blossom could use that. Not to worry, "We'll manage."

I returned to Scotland—in the seven days I'd been home, I realised what a responsibility I'd taken on—it was at that period I realised I was a boy no longer.

6

I MUST have been posted to twenty different aerodromes during the war years, but my happiest posting lasted for about three months when I was sent to London. The squad were billeted out near Kew Gardens and each morning we boarded a large lorry that took us to bombed houses in different parts of the East End.

I was doing a job that had nothing to do with my training as a mechanic: I helped to make the houses occupiable again. I was known as a "bodger". Discharged from the WAAF, Blossom was, by now, very pregnant. I managed to find a room to rent in a house near Kew Bridge. Coal was rationed so, to keep the home fire burning, I cut up timber from the bombing debris —I also supplied the landlady and a few other guests—so much did I bring back, the other boarders referred to me as Mr. Woodcock.

Being stationed in London gave me a

chance to offer my services at local pubs and clubs that provided live entertainment. The marriage allowance the RAF paid hardly bought the rations we were allocated. Evenings were free most days of the week but I would be placed on fire picket duty. The trouble with this was I wouldn't know which night until my name appeared on the duty roster; this happened about three times each ten days. It was about this time I began to understand how human nature works with different people.

The money I was making gave me a chance to provide many extras for Blossom. If I couldn't make the engagement, it meant the loss of a couple of quid, and you can guess the extra meat and orange juice I could buy with it, especially when you consider that my pay was only ten shillings a week.

I mentioned the dilemma to my pal Jimmy, a wide boy from Lewisham. He suggested I bribe the Flight Sergeant to take me off the roster. I had never learned how to do this so I "levelled" with the F/S. I told him I sometimes appeared at locals, and would he like to come with me one evening. To my surprise, he agreed. I took him to a pub called the Green Man at Leytonstone. I had done a few jobs there before and was fairly popular with the audience. He watched me perform and was quite surprised. Afterwards the customers, with that lovely London generosity they have, would offer us drinks. The F/S, who liked a pint or two, took all that was offered. I even gave him mine as I didn't touch the stuff. When we left, he was in a smiling mellow mood.

I explained on the train back to the billet that I was picking up an extra five or six pounds doing what I was doing. He slurred, "That's all right Max—I can fix it."

I told him I would give him a pound out of my wages if he could. He put his hand out, shook mine and said, "It's a deal!" Not only did he fix the roster, he also fixed up RAF transport to take me to the "gig".

Things were going sweetly when I had my first taste of that surprise in human nature I was mentioning. F/S cornered me one morning and quietly said that if he was caught doing what he was doing, he could be court-martialled. Therefore, he reckoned his fee should be doubled. It was blackmail, but I had to pay up. *The last I heard of F/S, he was working as a tax consultant somewhere in Nottingham.*

On 3 May 1943, our baby was born. We called her Christine. She was beautiful, she got "oohs" and "aahs" from the neighbours and I didn't get a good night's sleep for the rest of the time we were at Kew. I would fall asleep on the transporter through tiredness. Working all day and performing at night was turning me into a zombie. The pals I was with knew I was recently married and put it down to "too much". On top of all this, Adolf was sending the V2 rockets over; they were frightening, you didn't hear them until they exploded. Many of them were too close for comfort and Hitler looked as if he had found the secret weapon with which to win the war.

Because of the threat of invasion, I was posted to RAF Lympne down near Folkestone on the south coast. I didn't know it but that posting was to shape my whole life's pattern. Bloss, as I called her, left the digs at Kew, then moved to her sister's house at Dagenham. Her sister Evelyn

111

looked after Christine and Bloss took a job as a telephonist at the Rainham Telephone Exchange, where she earned £2.10s for a seven-day week.

She got plenty of dirty phone calls too —even in those times—one day she said, "Hello?" when a heavy breather said, "I know what you want—you want me to come where you live—break the door down—take you in the bedroom and make passionate love to you!"

Bloss, unruffled, said, "You can tell all this from just 'hello'?"

At Lympne, a notice appeared on the board for any talent to appear in a station concert competition; the winner would be sent to London to compete with other talent for the Hayes Cup, a wonderful silver trophy that would be awarded to the station for a complete year, when it would be competed for again. I put my name down, took part in the elimination, won it, and was given a pass to travel to RAF Uxbridge for the finals.

There were thirty finalists over two nights. On the third night, the top eight competed in a glittering show that was judged by some well-known names from show business—Mr. Ivor Novello, Miss Elizabeth Allen, a well-known actress, and Freddie Carpenter, one of the great stage directors.

I had extended my repertoire to include a mime of the way different people played darts. I also did an impression of an American group then becoming popular, known as The Inkspots, did my ace card—a Max Miller impression—and finished on the floor being weighed down by the microphone as I impersonated a new skinny singer from America they called Frank Sinatra. The cup was mine to take back to Lympne. I carried it there in a brown paper shopping bag with A. Powell, Family Butcher, printed on the side. I felt as if I had won the Lonsdale Belt.

The calls began to arrive at RAF Lympne for me to take part in many shows being produced in London. A regular caller was Flight Lieutenant Rex Harrison, who requested me for shows at the Nuffield Centre and hospitals at Roehampton. I even appeared in a show at the Drury Lane Theatre, the most frightening engagement I had ever appeared on. When the battery of lights went up and the spotlight picked me up from the corner to face almost three thousand people in the audience, together with the sound of a thirty-five piece orchestra playing my entrance music, I wanted to run and hide. The greatest number of people I had ever played to was about five or six hundred, the biggest band sound I had ever heard was a quintet—also, this audience had actually *paid* to come in. I survived and actually liked the sensation, even though it was the same feeling, I imagine, you got if you were going to the gallows.

7

EVENTUALLY, the war was over. The jubilation was short because we had to get back to mending the cities that were bombed, the lives that were shattered and "making homes fit for heroes", even if we were to call them pre-fabs. America had dropped two atom bombs on Japan, which nobody blamed them for because we didn't know the damage those things could do—what we *should* have blamed them for was, after knowing what devastation that first bomb made, they dropped a second—to my mind unforgiveable. It passed at the time almost unnoticed because of our eagerness to see the street lights on again.

Evelyn, Blossom's sister, wanted the room back because her husband had returned from the army. We had to find some place to live with two-year-old Christine in tow, and not many people wanted to rent rooms to a young couple with an infant. After weeks of searching, we found a couple of rooms not too far from Plumstead Common, rented to us by a publican, a very nice man named Sid Carter. I had been given a demob suit that wasn't all that good a fit—in fact, when I wore it to an agent's office, he thought I was a Shakesperian actor wearing my costume for Richard the Third. Clothing was still rationed on coupons, but I bought a dinner jacket with shiny lapels from a second-hand shop in Little Newport Street, just off Charing Cross Road. They supplied waiters, but by the time Blossom had made a few alterations to the trousers and put some shoulder-pads in the jacket, it had a pretty good shape. This was my working attire for the gigs I hoped to get as a semi-pro. The suit, shirt, bow tie and patent shoes cost £2.15s. I used them for the next three years.

There were variety theatres around London where agents gathered in the hope of spotting "potential". One of these was the Grand Theatre at Clapham. I worked there and was spotted by a small-time agent named Gordon Norval, a kindly man who ran an agency with his wife in Charing Cross Road.

I forget how I got the date at Clapham but I know I was paid £11 for the week. Mr. Norval liked what he saw, then gave me six weeks at different theatres in and around London; they were "number three" dates, which included the Hippodrome, Poplar; Hippodrome, Aldershot; Kilburn and three others. I was always second act to go on—this, because a stand-up front-cloth act was needed while the scene shifters dressed the stage for the next act that usually required a full set. They mostly wanted no more than eight minutes —ten at the most—and woe betide you if the allotted time was exceeded. *A manager at one theatre would wait until an act walked on the stage Monday night, then he'd walk out of the theatre, cross the road —he would stand there—if he couldn't hear the audience applauding—you didn't work there again. I had a bit of luck—he got run over.*

I threw myself into the business of entertaining. During the war years I had performed at hundreds of concerts, also made many personal appearances. Apart from taking part in sketches—painting scenery—working the light switchboard—acting as compère—singing popular songs and being general dogsbody, I had a fair idea of the economics that must go hand in hand with successful production. I was almost ready to turn pro.

For a few months as a civilian, I worked back in the building trade—for a forty-hour week my take-home pay was a little over £5. I could get that for a fifteen-minute act at one of the British Legion clubs. It didn't need a genius to know which direction to take. *"Oh, he's going into show business," wailed my mother— "... all those orgies—all those drugs— all those scantily dressed women...!" Grandad, sitting in the corner also wailing: "Take me—take me!"*

I had been assured by some Australian Servicemen I had served with that there was a great deal of show business going on in their part of the world; almost every city had two or three well-equipped theatres. Young and full of adventure, Blossom and I decided to apply for the £10 assisted passage to that far-away land, as it was then. We queued with hundreds of others outside Australia House in the Strand to fill in the forms and take the medical. With just about three more couples in front of us, they closed the doors with a "Come back tomorrow".

On the train back to the cold and draughty rooms at Plumstead, we made up our minds to get up as early as possible, give Christine her breakfast, then travel up again to the Strand. That night, I had to comfort Bloss about pulling up our roots and try to convince her that if I made good out there, we would be able to afford return travel and see our families. I felt the tears on her cheek and wondered whether I was making the right decision.

We rose early, I put my grey pinstripe demob suit on, a fresh white shirt with sober tie, polished my shoes and as Jack the Lad, prepared to become a fair dinkum Aussie. As we closed the door, walking up the path towards us came the postman. He had a letter in his hand addressed to me. It was from the BBC. About a month previously, I had attended an audition for the Beeb. I had heard nothing and assumed they were not interested. I had given them my sister-in-law, Evelyn's, address and that's where the letter had gone. She had readdressed it to Plumstead. I opened it and read that they would like to see me back at Aeolian Hall in Bond Street at 2.30 that very afternoon. All thoughts of Australia vanished. I think Bloss was secretly relieved because it was only to please me she had gone along with the Australian venture. *I didn't mind too much either, having to go through that sheep dip had never appealed.*

At two-thirty prompt, I presented the letter to the commissionaire at Aeolian Hall, was shown up to a studio and asked to repeat the audition I had done previously. They liked it, I was booked for a series of programmes to be called *They're Out*. The show featured ex-Servicemen who had a spark of talent the Beeb hoped to foster. There were lots of us; names like Spike Milligan, Jimmy Edwards, Frankie Howerd, Harry Secombe, Benny Hill and many, many more took part. It was an opportunity I grabbed with both hands. In those radio days, you could be heard by as many as thirty million listeners. If you "took", it was a short cut to stardom.

One programme was heard by band-leader Jack Payne, who had become a producer of shows for the theatre. He sent a representative with the unlikely name of Scruffy Dale to see me work at the Nuffield Centre. Dale reckoned I would be okay for a show that was shortly to go into production called *For the Fun of It*, starring Donald Peers and Nosmo King. Nosmo was a raconteur who had made his name up from a NO SMOKING sign.

With another unknown, Frankie Howerd, I signed a contract to tour with the show for the next sixteen weeks. We would go to all the Number One Moss Empire dates, something most pros dreamed of but few attained, yet here I was making my first long tour at the cream of British theatres. Also I was to get £15 per week—for me a fortune!

Jack Payne was a bullying sort of man —I can never remember him smiling, he never gave a compliment and very little pleased him. He would find fault with the sixteen John Tiller Girls that made up the chorusline, the musicians he treated like dirt, even Donald Peers, who was the star attraction, came in for a lot of stick. When this man came into a theatre we were working, Frankie Howerd and I made ourselves scarce. JP was slow to recognise Frankie Howerd's talent. Frank was unique and some places we went to didn't understand what he was getting at. At Sunderland Empire, one restless customer in the gallery threw a large shipbuilding rivet on to the stage during Frank's act. If it had hit him, it could have killed him. When JP saw this reaction, he would talk about severing Frank's contract. Howerd was so highly strung he would walk the streets until the early hours worrying about it. Luckily, many people recognised his original approach and it was only a matter of two more years before he was a household name and Payne was taking the credit for discovering him. He also got Frank on a contract that was only just short of criminal—at one time, Frankie told me, the Jack Payne office were taking seventy-five per cent of the money he earned—it came to many thousands.

It doesn't cause all that much eyebrow-raising today because the predators ripping off youngsters in rock groups are legendary—these days, they pass themselves off as "management"—when Frank and I were greenhorns they were known as "greedy bastards".

The cartoon character of a theatrical agent is usually a ruthless, cigar-smoking, Jewish scalper, who is in it for the money. About that time, I met agent Jock Jacobsen. Jock was Jewish but totally different from the image used in *Punch*, or magazines like that. Jock was a quiet, unassuming man, with a nice sense of humour. He had been a drummer with the Lew Stone Band. After leaving the RAF as a bandsman, Jock, with a partner named Norman Payne, formed a theatrical agency. I met Jock, liked him immensely and signed with his office for him to represent me. I would pay him ten per cent of all I made. It was an agreement that was to last for more than thirty years.

Not only did Jock manage me—he was my greatest fan and in his quiet way "sold" me to managements that I was new to. He once booked me to a theatre in Jersey; because of the booking, I had to cancel a date at a social club in Hillingdon, near Uxbridge. This club belonged to an operator known as Johnny Kelly, and we have kept in touch over the years. He now lives in Worthing in West Sussex. Last year, when I was appearing in a concert there, Johnny came backstage to say hello and produced a letter I had written to him *forty* years before. It was held together by Sellotape because he had shown it to so many people over the years it was falling apart. It read:

August 18th, 1947

Dear Johnny:

I have been contracted to perform in Jersey on the date you mention so will be unable to help you.

May I suggest an act who I feel sure will please your audience, his name is Benny Hill. He will do it for £2.10s. for the night—I know you won't be disappointed.

See you when I return.

Regards.

Max.

As Johnny was putting the letter back in

his wallet, I asked, "Did you ever use Benny?"

Johnny laughed. "No bloody fear—he was too expensive."

I don't think I have ever mentioned this story to Benny Hill who, with his successful television shows running all over the world must be one of the richest performers ever to come out of that era. He is such a big television star—today, when one watches his shows on the box it is hard to imagine that he, like all of us then, was floundering about trying to make a crust.

The words "West End nightclub" conjure up images of women in fashionable clothes —men in tuxedos and the popping of champagne corks, the glitter of the décor as the waiters glide across reflected dance floors in time to the orchestra led by a debonair conductor in immaculate tails— is what the "B" movies usually convey— the West End nightclubs I was employed at were little more than upholstered sewers; they were always in basements and badly lit. *I worked at a place so dark, one waiter had a guide dog—the menu was in*

Braille—a customer asked the maître d' *if he had any vintage brandy, the* maitre d' *said, "No, but hang on, I'll make you some!" A passerby asked the doorman if they had any Bunny Girls down there. He said, "No, but you should see the size of the rats." The kitchen was run by the Mafia—you daren't mention the word "chicken", the chef took it personally.*

All the above patter I put into my act later on in life; had I attempted to work it during those immediate post-war days I'd have been thrown out of the joint by bouncers. The owners cherished these places, they competed for trade among other owners of clubs that were mushrooming in every little alley and side-street in the West End.

Two clubs that were a cut above the Soho rubbish were run by a man named Harry Adams. He had a good eye for fresh talent on the scene. Harry owned a place in Windmill Street, right opposite the "We Never Closed" theatre. A similar place was behind Liberty's in Regent Street, another subterranean joint known as The Blue Lagoon. It was rare for the owners to pay acts more than £15 for the week. Another rip-off we performers could do nothing about was to "double", play both clubs in the same night but, the owners, instead of paying £15 for each venue, got together to pay £25 for both. On top of this, they usually looked to the agent to "kick back" half the commission they were taking from the act—oh yes, we had to learn it the hard way. Difficult to imagine when one thinks the hostesses were getting customers to order inferior champagne at £10 a bottle and that customers' bills sometimes exceeded £100—how could anybody pinch a couple of quid from performers that needed it more—but they did.

During my early days, I met another performer who was booked to "double" with me at The Blue Lagoon and The Panama Club. He was an enormous, good-natured fellow who became a friend for life. He did a conjuring act; his name, Tommy Cooper.

The dressing room we shared was no bigger than a telephone kiosk, and in this Tommy also had to "load" his tricks. He would go on first and I would follow. While I was on, Tommy would have gathered his tricks together, re-loaded, then made his way from the Blue Lagoon to The Panama, a distance of about a quarter of a mile. I was all right because I would grab my top coat and run the few hundred yards, but Tommy had two suitcases full of tricks, and it wasn't easy.

One Friday night when business was booming at both places, I arrived at the second club to find the cabaret hadn't started. The owner, Harry Adams, looking most indignant, greeted me with, "Where's the big bloke?", meaning Tommy.

"He left well before me, he should be here," I told the boss.

Adams said, "You'd better get on first —tell the band to change the running order." I did this. I also had no idea where Tommy had got to—the discipline in show business was so strict then that possibly the greatest breach a performer could commit was not be on time.

Half-way through my Sinatra spoof, I saw the shadowy figure of Tommy sneak in behind the spotlight a waiter was operating, then prepare to follow my session. I waited around because the all-night bus

128

didn't leave Trafalgar Square until 3 a.m. so I had lots of time on my hands. Tommy took his applause, then when he came off I asked the reason for his lateness.

He explained that when he left The Blue Lagoon with his two suitcases, a policeman stopped him and wanted to know what somebody was doing with two heavy suitcases after midnight, walking past Garrard's—Jewellers to His Majesty.

Tommy told the copper he was a conjuror who was working the clubs and was on his way to perform. The policeman, not satisfied with Tom's story, asked him to open the cases. Tommy took up the story from there . . .

"I opened the case—the copper looked at the silver rings, together with the bright vases I use in the act—then he told me he was an amateur conjuror himself and wanted me to convince him that I could do the tricks and that I hadn't stolen the cases—so there I was, in the middle of Regent Street at one o'clock in the morning, doing bottle—glass—glass— bottle—bottle—glass—etc." It was after that the policeman told him he could go.

I was to meet Tommy time and time again through our careers, each time with hilarious results. I'll tell you more later.

8

ALMOST at the same time as I started the tour with *For the Fun of It*, Blossom informed me that she was infanticipating once more. For a few weeks, she brought Christine on tour. We played cities around England, Scotland and Wales. As soon as landladies saw the three of us enter their digs at the beginning of the week, they weren't enamoured of the idea, especially as Blossom swelled up enormously during pregnancy. When we handed our ration books to the lady of the house, she usually took them reluctantly, but somehow they stood for it. I suppose they thought it was only for a week, it wasn't for ever.

Theatrical artistes like to sleep late—children wake early, so one of us would take turns walking young Christine out to the nearest park playground, sitting her on the swings or roundabout, trying to make the hours pass till lunch-time. When we returned, we were so hungry we would eat like navvies. *We had one landlady who was very fond of cats—we would only eat the vegetables!*

Then, like manna from Heaven, we were told we had been granted a council house on a new estate just outside Romford. We had put our name down two years previously, never dreaming we would be lucky. It was one of the happiest days we had known. For twenty-five shillings a week, we moved into a new three-bedroom house with a large garden, dream kitchen and all mod cons. All the good things began to happen at once: Bloss gave birth to a nine-pound boy we named Anthony. Jock Jacobsen had got my fee raised from £15 a week to £35—a very big wage in those days—and I was booked for three movies to be made at Bushey.

The first two films I made were for a producer named Arthur Dent, a respected movie-maker from Wardour Street, who was notorious for his strict budget. I was playing the second lead to Hal Monty, a "business" comic—for this I was paid £50 for the week, then I landed the part of coachman in *Tom Brown's Schooldays*.

From all this, I bought my first car on

hire purchase, a Ford Anglia, GUF 650, paid £450 for it, took my test in Cambridge at twelve noon, just as the undergrads were racing off to lunch. You have never seen so many bicycles—it looked like Shanghai when the work day is over. The examiner must have thought he was testing a bulldozer-driver, so much did I brake and start—he passed me—I think he was glad to get out. I loved the car as a man can love only his first—I would polish it morning, noon and night.

Through touring so much, I had very little chance to get to know our neighbours. I was known to most of them as I was broadcasting for the BBC. Mine was the only car in the street. Imagine then, one morning coming out with my tin of Simoniz and finding the bonnet and mudguards scraped with a nail, unbelievably vandalised. *Later, I said to my brother, "Who could have done such a thing?" Harry's only reply was, "They must have heard you sing."*
Food, sweets, clothes, petrol and furniture were still strictly rationed and would be for several more years. The black-out

had been lifted but that was about the only bonus the British people were able to enjoy. Their chief source of entertainment was the cinema or the variety theatre; it was boom-time for managements. Jock booked me in to a touring revue, *Fine Feathers Make Fine Birds*. The producer was another Payne, Ernie Payne. My money had risen to £60 a week; he suggested that as I didn't have a bank account, I should only take half my salary and let him look after the rest until the tour was over. This I agreed to. At the end of the ten-week tour, Ernie vanished into thin air and so did my savings. You pay for experience. Come to think of it, I was "conned" several times during my early years; some I won, some I lost.

Rest assured, if you have a pound or two, somebody is going to try and have it. I remember once in the early Sixties, a respected member of the Variety Club was working for John Bloom, the washing machine tycoon. His name was Andy Neatroux. I believe he was innocent of what he did. He called me and the conversation went like this:

Andy: Max, good morning, Andy here . . .

Me: Hello Andy—what can I do for you?

Andy: Max, you know I represent John Bloom; well, John is launching a new company called English and Overseas Investments but he'd like only his friends to have shares—friends like Bernard Delfont—Jack Hylton—Val Parnell and yourself.

Me: (Flattered at being mentioned in such illustrious company) OK Andy—include me in (Greed coming to the fore). How many can I have?

Andy: Only a thousand per person.

Me: I'll send you a cheque.

The next week, the shares plummeted from £1.40 to 3 pence—John Bloom was declared bankrupt. The share certificate is now mounted in my office as a reminder to beware of get-rich-quick schemes.

Another "con", one that turned out right for me, was also in the early Sixties. It was from Lionel Bart, and I feel sure he won't mind me telling this.

Lionel came to my office with a cassette

of songs, sixteen in all, for a new musical he had written to be called *Oliver!* I had already made a big winner on Decca Records of one of his previous compositions, "Fings ain't wot they use t'be". He told me he had received an offer of £300 for the score but if I could better it, my company, Lakeview Music, could be the publishers. The only song I liked in the entire score was "Consider Yourself". I agreed to pay him £350 for the rights. I recorded "Consider Yourself", which was a huge success, then got Shirley Bassey to record another Number One, "As long as He Needs Me". The show was a worldwide hit. A few years later, I sold my company to an American publishing house, known as Essex Music. Jock Jacobsen, who did most of the business dealing, and I became very prosperous; alas, poor old Lionel Bart could never hold on to his windfall. Lionel, who is generous to a fault, watched it all slip through his fingers, then the dreaded taxman demanded his cut. Lionel is a lovely kind man, I feel sure there are some more hit songs lurking inside him. I feel sure too, that Lionel some day will erupt again. By the way, he also told me later that he never had an offer of £300—he invented that to get an extra fifty quid out of me.

Before I leave the "con" game, maybe I can benefit the reader with one more story: my accountant took me to see some young executives who had started a tax avoidance business. Their office was right next door to the Ritz Hotel in Piccadilly, glamorous receptionists welcomed us with coffee and liqueurs. We were ushered into a walnut-panelled office with Connolly hide armchairs, where sat a young executive in blue shirt with white collar, Christian Dior striped suit and cowboy-style boots. He promised that by "straddling" commodities, he could make our money work for us better than any other investment in the money market. I parted with £20,000 and that went the same way as Ernie Payne.

When Dennis Healey, the then Chancellor of the Exchequer, heard about the scheme, he brought out a tax reform that backdated two years. When I asked the accountant where he had heard of these money wizards he said, "I forget." I don't go near the markets any more. Since the crash in October 1987, I realise how devious money managers can be. With a minimum of knowledge, a person can start a scheme where he or she can easily persuade a gullible investor to part with savings—it's all right when the market holds steady, but come a bad period, shares are wiped out and the poor old investor takes the loss. I have yet to find anywhere safer than the interest paid at the High Street bank. Unless the ads state in bold black type that "markets can go down *and* often do!" I don't think Sunday papers should accept the advertisement.

Back to the late Forties where the last thing on my mind was the stock market. Every waking hour I spent assiduously working at my chosen profession, showbiz. There were very few known script writers at that time; in fact, I had heard of only one—that was Ted Kavanagh of ITMA fame. I noticed that Frankie Howerd, by now the most popular comedian on radio, had ideas and routines that were new and unique. Having spent many months sharing dressing rooms and boarding houses with Frank, I knew that the output of material he was using must be supplied by some other source. I asked Frank who was supplying this material and whether I would be able to buy some scripts from him myself. He told me the provider was a chap about my own age named Eric Sykes, a young man from Oldham in Lancashire. He also told me that if I cared to come to the Camberwell Palace the following Sunday night, after *Variety Band Box* had gone off the air, I could meet Eric because, as it was the end of a series, there was to be a party given by the BBC. I turned up with Blossom after the show. Frank's dressing room was full of well-wishers congratulating him on another superb broadcast; we thought it was the wrong time and we'd better leave.

Blossom decided she would like to use the ladies' toilet before we journeyed back to Romford in the little Anglia. She entered and came out again almost immediately. "What's the matter?" I asked.

She said there was a chap in the loo being violently sick—she'd have to wait until he came out as she couldn't make the journey back to Romford without spending a penny.

A few minutes later, this pasty-faced fellow emerged with a big smile and said, "It's all yours." He bowed low and almost lost his balance. I caught him. He said, "Thanks mate," then introduced himself. "I'm Eric Sykes—and I write funny words." He wrote his address down on a piece of newspaper; he lived in one room in Earls Court Road. He also gave me his landlady's phone number to leave a message if I thought we could do something together. He confided that he was quite broke now that *Variety Band Box* had finished.

That was forty years ago and we have remained friends ever since. There's hardly a week goes by when we don't play a game of golf, or call each other, sometimes from the other side of the world— very often with the latest jokes . . . *Hey Max—hear about the fellow in bed with the girl—in the middle of their lovemaking she asks the bloke, "You haven't got Aids, have you?" The bloke says, "No." She says, "Good, 'cos I don't want to go through that again!"*

Eric later confessed that the reason he was so drunk on the night of the party at

Camberwell Palace was because he had been refused a credit as the writer of Howerd's material either at the end of the broadcast or in the *Radio Times*. He was being paid only £5 for these hilarious ideas so he figured he would take some of his fee in drink. That was the reason he was vomiting down the pan in the Ladies.

Shortly after that, I visited his one room in Earls Court. When I got there, he was boiling an egg—he asked if I would like a cup of tea. I said I would. He then said could I wait until his egg boiled because he only had one saucepan and no teapot. You haven't lived unless you've had a cup of tea with eggshell in. *Hey Eric, hear about the old fellow that goes to the brothel—the madam says, "How old are you?" He tells her he is ninety-two. She says, "Grandpa, you've had it!" He says, "Really, how much do I owe you?"*

Eric wrote some great routines for the Palladium shows I appeared in. I don't think there are too many writers, even today, with his off-beat imagination—to me he is superb.

9

THE touring continued, but with a place of our own it was good to get home, even for a few hours. The little Anglia, after the last performance on Saturday evening, had to be pushed through the night, at times for a couple of hundred miles, then on Monday morning probably two hundred more to a variety theatre somewhere up north. Petrol was not easy to come by, unless you found a friendly garage man or somebody on the bill hadn't used up all their ration coupons.

Once I travelled through the night from Bath to London; after the show a dancer appearing on the bill at the Theatre Royal there asked for a lift. His act was billed as McAndrews and Miles, "From Ballet to Tap". Keith McAndrews was the dancer, now a very successful promoter of shows around Britain. We see quite a lot of each other these days, if there is a listener Keith loves to tell this story . . .

In those days, he had a bad stammer that he has now conquered but back in the Fifties he found it hard to put two words together. Half-way to London, I noticed the petrol gauge reading "empty". Garages did not stay open in those days but in some cases a garage had a bell lit by a dim light. If you rang this bell the proprietor would come out to serve you.

There wasn't a living soul in the streets and I began to get worried about making it to Romford. It was a bitterly cold night, then as we neared Beaconsfield, I suddenly spied a figure huddled up walking with head down against the wind. I pulled over towards him and, forgetting Keith's stuttering, I said, "Ask that chap if he knows where there's a garage?"

Keith rolled the window down and stammered, "Do—you—know—where we we we might f f f find—a—garage?"

The man said, "G g g go up—up the r r road . . ."

The only human being we had seen for miles and miles and we had found another stammerer. Keith smiles about it now but he says he was afraid the chap was going to give him one for taking the micky.

We still talk about the boarding houses, and the landladies who were a breed of their own. They were mostly kindhearted souls who looked forward to the comings and goings of theatrical people to relieve the monotony of living alone—usually widows who supplemented their pensions by renting a room or two. They worked hard at getting you to return next time you toured that way because the competition among other landladies looking for custom was intense.

I recall one landlady in Leeds who promised that when we returned the whole place would be refurbished. "Eee—I'm going to have Regency flock wallpaper on the walls—crushed velvet curtains at the windows and across the top I'm having a *pelvis.*"

On one occasion, Frankie Howerd, I and a pianist who accompanied Donald Peers, stayed together at digs in Sheffield. The pianist, Ernest Ponticelli, had a birthday. The sixteen Tiller Girls clubbed together to buy him a bottle of sherry,

which he shared with Frank and me—
every night, after the show, we would each
have a small wineglassful.

Towards the end of the week, the sherry
had diminished considerably. Ernie
guessed that the landlady had been having
a swig. We finished up what remained,
then took the bottle into the bathroom and
pee-ed into it—just a small amount—and
left it on the sideboard.

The next day we spent giggling like
schoolgirls at the shock the landlady was
going to receive. We arrived back after the
show and had a good supper which the
landlady asked if we enjoyed. We told her
it was excellent, hardly able to keep
straight faces at the thought of her
swallowing the contents of the bottle,
which had gone down a good inch.

In the next breath she said, "I hope you
didn't mind, I used a little of your sherry
for the trifle." The smiles left our faces
and I have never touched sherry to this
day.

Thanks to Eric Sykes' scripts and an original line in comedy, it wasn't long before
I was back on the Moss Empire circuit. I

was engaged to appear at the Glasgow Empire—a nightmare for English comedians—Dickie Henderson used to say, "If they like you in Glasgow, they don't applaud—they let you live!"

Well, in Glasgow, they not only let me live, they applauded and whistled for encores. This was noted by the then Czar of show business, Val Parnell. Glasgow was a constant headache to him. As a booking, most talking acts gave excuses like other dates, or dental appointments. When it came to his ears that a London comedian had moved the granite faces that were regulars each week, he became interested.

The following week I was due to appear at Finsbury Park Empire in north London. Val Parnell made it his business to travel out to see me. He must have been impressed because he came backstage, climbed the stairs to the dressing room, shook my hand and told me we would be seeing a lot of each other in the future.

Things happened far more quickly than I could have imagined. On the Thursday of that week, Ted Ray, a very popular comedian at the Palladium, had to beg off

—it was a matinée day—which meant an afternoon show plus two evening shows. Parnell arranged for me to take Ted Ray's place at the Palladium for the three shows —I also had to carry on at Finsbury Park. So, on that eventful day in May 1951 I was shuttled from Oxford Circus to Finsbury Park, where I completed five shows in one day.

On the bill at the Palladium was Hollywood film star, Dorothy Lamour. I preceded her and, as the band played her entrance music, "Moon of Manakoora," she was kind enough to wait in the wings to press my hands and whisper, "Great!" There's no need to tell you that as I drove the Anglia towards Romford that night, I could have been arrested for flying.

Val Parnell decided that I was to cancel the dates I had in my engagement book, so that I could be included on Palladium bills that were topped mostly by American performers.

My first-ever date was with the Hollywood duo Abbott and Costello. I couldn't get to know Bud Abbott but Lou Costello and I got on like a house on fire. I was surprised how little he and his partner conversed—they only seemed to speak on the stage, then left the theatre separately without even saying goodnight to each other. Lou didn't seem to care about anything except having a good time; if somebody approached him about almost anything he'd say, "Speak to my manager". When I read in *Variety* that Lou had passed away almost penniless, owing great sums to the Inland Revenue, having got through millions of dollars at the race-track and on wild living, I felt very sad for him, very sad indeed.

I didn't guess at that period of my life the famous theatre, the Palladium, was to become my home for the next ten years. I was to appear there in no fewer than four-teen different shows. I love the Palladium; it is a performer's dream, for a stand-up act it is hard to fail—but it isn't all that good a place to present sketches because if the action takes place more than six feet from the edge of the apron it doesn't work. But for extravaganza and personality, it is the best in the world. *I met this fellow, he said, "I'm going to the London Plasma to see the show." I said, "Plasma? You mean*

Palladium—plasma's blood." He said, "Seven shillings for a stalls seat—what's that?"

In the early Fifties, there were still more than two hundred variety theatres functioning up and down the country; there was little need to change your act because every week was a different audience. Indeed, it was very hard to change even if you wanted to. Once the act had been approved by the head office, you were expected to keep to the same jokes, the same songs and the same time on stage. Your contract usually read "as known". You were expected to provide band parts for each member of the orchestra, always to be immaculately turned out, even if you did a "tramp" act the props you wore had to be clean so as not to offend patrons in the stalls. You were also expected to supply the theatre with half a dozen ten-by-eight glossy pictures of yourself.

It was possible to tour for two or three years without going back to the same audience. In London alone there were twenty or more theatres, so with pantomime and summer season, a good act could work for the rest of its life without altering one word—and many did. Television was to change all that, but these were early days, very few managements attached any importance to the "goggle-box", very few realised how it was to turn their Palaces into bingo halls, but it did, it was to close all those variety theatres and Odeons like a plague.

Of course, the early Fifties audiences were still being entertained by steam radio, what's more the Beeb was leading the world in radio production—still is. I entered the radio scene as a regular in a show to be titled *Educating Archie*. The star was a ventriloquist's dummy. *I saw Archie quite recently, he didn't look at all well—Dutch Elm Disease.*

Eric Sykes had always been amused by my impersonation of Arthur Dent, the movie producer. I had made films for him a few years previously—Eric's favourite piece was when I'd explain that the director would ask for another "take", and extra takes in films cost money and time. Mr. Dent would suddenly step forward from behind the camera, then in a very thick accent say, "No—don't do another take—there was a little bit of magic in that last take that you will never recapture— now be guided by me and move on to the next shot!"

When Eric was asked to write *Educating Archie*, he remembered the impression. He plugged for me to play the part of Archie's tutor, which from day one was an enormous success and would be for the next few years, picking up many awards along the way. He found the character I was portraying very warm and funny—so did the listening audience, from the moment the character entered with "I've arrived and to prove it I'm 'ere!" the fun started.

Archie: I've never been on safari, Mr. Bygraves.

Max: Stay close to me son and you'll be safe.

Archie: I've been told that if a leopard approaches, you wait until you can see the eyes then shoot between them.

Max: No, they're wise to that son—they walk around in twos with one eye closed.

With *Educating Archie* I became a radio personality. The show was popular with children, we had a listening audience of twenty-five million and my position on variety bills was elevated. And, like most performers from humble beginnings, I wanted the comforts that go hand in hand with all this.

The first step was to own my own house —we gave up the council house in Romford and moved to north London, a sensible address because most of the work was north of Edgware and it took a good hour off journeys by car to places like Manchester, Leeds and Birmingham. The house cost £3,000, which I took a mortgage on. Taxation was very high and I wasn't sure how long it would be before the bubble burst.

I had made my first Royal Command Performance before King George VI and Queen Elizabeth, now Queen Mum. I had supported acts like Donald Peers and Judy Garland at the Palladium and was becoming, what I am reluctant to say—a personality. I was making so much money, I didn't think there was that much "bread" in the world—and it tasted good.

The work was enjoyable but physically it was tiring. Luckily I can sleep at the drop of an eyelid so my batteries were easily recharged. Eric Sykes, who has trouble sleeping, has often said to me that if he could trade places with anybody it would be me, just to be able to sleep as I do.

It may surprise some to know that at this time in my career, I did very little singing in my act. I had written up an idea based on all the Frankie Laine hits—I mixed up songs like "Riders in the Sky", "Rawhide", "Shrimp Boats", and others. It was a big success as a piece of stage material. When a man named Wally Ridley of EMI Records heard it, he said I should record it. I did, and it went into the very first Record Top Ten that was ever compiled—it stayed for many weeks. I called it "The Cowpunchers Cantata".

Wally was managing Peter Brough at the time and began looking for unusual titles for me to record. (I once recorded a song, "You're a Pink Toothbrush—I'm a Blue Toothbrush". At the time I thought it was a song for the listening children—now they've grown up and taught it to their

children—it has sold over ten million—
not records—toothbrushes!)

I recorded some unbelievable titles:
"When You Come to the End of a
Lollipop"; "Gilly Gilly Ossenfeffer
Katzenellen Bogan by the Sea"; "Big
Head"; "Put Away the Chip Chopper
Charlie"; "What Noise Annoys an Oyster"
and many more. Strangely enough, they all
sold very well, mostly because I was the
only one covering that part of the record
market. EMI recently reissued an album
filled with those titles. Sykes once sent me
a printed copy of a song, "I Haven't had
a Bang Since Bonfire Night". Goodness
knows who dreamed that one up.

In the midst of all this, we had another
daughter, a beautiful young lady whom my
wife decided to call Maxine. She was born
at our new home in north London.
Engagements were still far from home,
with Maxine only a few months old we
moved to Brighton for a summer show.

I appeared in the record-breaking show *A
Good Idea Son* at the Hippodrome,
Brighton. It was there I got to know two
charming hoteliers named Lil and Al Feld.

Al had worked his way up from a violin player with the Palais band to owning a small hotel in Regency Square. After the show, several of our cast would congregate in the Beach Club below the hotel, have sandwiches, a drink and a laugh—almost every night. Al swears that from this enterprise and the customers that came in for the free entertainment, he moved on to a bigger hotel; the Norfolk. They bought several others and now they have a large chain of them. So successful was Al that he became Mayor of Brighton. He and Lil worked hard for every penny they earned. When Al took on the big hotel, both he and Lil wondered whether they had done the sensible thing. A few of the show business crowd made it their meeting-place on a Sunday morning. With Stan on piano, it took off as the most popular bar in Brighton and the Felds never looked back. I cannot help remembering that bar without thinking of the Coopers, Tommy and his wife Dove, who made it their local on Sunday mornings.

One Sunday, they had a domestic upset —it happened because Tommy wasn't hurrying; she had a taxi waiting as they were living in Eastbourne, twenty miles away, and neither of them drove because it would restrict their drinking. Dove bullied him to hurry, one word led to another, she went off in a huff, got in the taxi, then left Tommy to make his own arrangements.

Fifteen minutes later, Tommy ordered another cab, then followed on. A small crowd of us, including Dove, sat around with our drinks chatting and listening to Stan playing some popular melodies. When Tommy's cab was five minutes away from the Norfolk, he stripped off his trousers and shirt, paid the driver, walked into the hotel with jacket, pants and shirt over his arm—on through the vestibule in his longjohns and suspenders, the Britishers roaring their heads off, the overseas visitors, who didn't know him from Adam, just gulping. Tommy walked into the bar, straight up to our table, waited for the laughter to die, then said, "Dove— where's my clean shirt?"

Dove had to forget their argument and laugh along with the others, but not before she got in, "You bloody idiot!"

10

IT was during this period I had a phone call from America that was to change many things. I had earlier that year appeared for a season at the Palladium as a supporting act to the great Judy Garland. Over the phone she—Judy—asked me if I could appear with her at the Palace Theatre in Times Square, New York. Judy had been a smash hit in London, now her husband-to-be, Sid Luft, decided she could storm New York in the same way. I told Jock about the phone call and he got on to New York and did a deal. I was to be paid $2,500 a week, we were to open on 16 October (my 29th birthday) for a three-week stint.

Although I was making good money, I had never collected that sort of loot in Britain. I had a few sleepless nights wondering whether I could do a stand-up act in front of an American audience. I was as Cockney as jellied eels and the thought of being the first vaudeville performer to leave these shores since Harry Lauder filled me with trepidation. "What the hell . . ." said Jock, ". . . they can't shoot us." So we went.

The take-off from London Airport, as it was then called, set my heart beating. Although I had been with the RAF for five years, the most I had flown was round the aerodrome on test flights. I had never been up at night. My first look at the lights below twinkling in amber and white was a revelation; the propellers of the plane were loud, but they didn't worry Jock or me; we were both as excited as children going to Disneyland.

In those days, the maximum amount allowed to be taken out of the UK in sterling was £25. Although we had applied for more business allowance, it had not come through. When we landed in New York, after paying the taxi off and tipping the bellboys, then meeting the bill in a restaurant, we had very little left, and pay-day was more than ten days off.

I still didn't know if I was going to be a success. Americans were ruthless about paying performers off if they didn't click, so we had to tread warily. Here we were, both comparatively well-off men, having to live on bowls of soup and biscuits for several days, then count the dollars to see if we could afford breakfast. When Sid Luft invited us to dinner a few days before the opening, we were both so hungry we made sparks come from the knives and forks.

The opening night at the Palace was a gala affair; big names from show business turned up in droves: Ethel Merman, Eddie Cantor, Jack Benny, Jackie Gleason, George Burns, Clark Gable, Frank Sinatra, Elizabeth Taylor, so many many more. I was to close the first half, the first talking act of the evening . . . *Good evening ladies and gentlemen—my name is Max Bygraves—there will be a pause while you say, "Who?" I've been worried ever since we landed on the runway at Idlewild Airport—we came by boat! A customs man came up to me and patted me on the back—and the front and down the sides. "What are you doing in the United States?" he asked. I said, "I've come to get away from it all!" He said, "You've come to the right place—there's none of it here . . ."*

I was getting laughs—I went into my bucket and mop routine—into the "Cowpunchers Cantata"—into the paper-tearing routine—into a "cod" Al Jolson impression:

Mammy—it's your little Sammy
Mammy, I know this is hammy
But I'm in a jammy—Mammy.

My fifteen minutes was over, generous applause—not show-stopping, but enough to tell me I hadn't failed. Of course everybody was waiting for the star. When she appeared, she *did* stop the show. After "We're a Couple of Swells" in tramp outfit, she could do no wrong. I was proud to be on the same stage as the great Judy Garland.

The three weeks we were booked for was extended to six, then eight, then ten weeks. I sent to London for Blossom: she joined me at the Park Sheraton Hotel on Central Park and we became a coupla New Yorkers for a while.

The agency looking after Judy Garland was the William Morris Agency; it was run by a man named Abe Lastfogel and after my opening night, his wife Fran approached me. She said that she thought I was wrong to "cod" Al Jolson. He had died recently and was revered by Americans; she almost commanded me to replace it with something else. I did as she requested but was never all that happy with my finish.

Judy was the sort of person who got easily bored with routine—it was not long before she was having late lunches, then arriving at the theatre to make her entrance by a hair's-breadth. She had agents, hairdressers and stage staff pacing the floor wondering what had happened to her.

One Wednesday afternoon, I was just finishing my act to a packed audience; as I took my final bow I was greeted in the wings by Ernest Adler, Judy's hairdresser, who had taken over as agent, stage manager and Judy's minder.

"Get back on stage and stall for as long as you can," said Ernie. He added, "Judy's not well."

I walked back on stage, after five seconds in the wings, then said to the audience, "I was sitting in my hotel room when I got a message to say you were still applauding . . ." They were a good-natured crowd so I filled in with every routine I knew—talked about rationing in England, talked about the war . . . "We had to wear gas-masks all through the day and night—we've got a fellow lives next door to us still hasn't told his mother-in-law the war is over."

I worked every gag I could, but each time I looked into the wings Ernie was opening and closing his arms, meaning "stretch it". By now, most of the William Morris Agency had left their offices, a short distance from the Palace, to see what was going on, among them Mrs. Lastfogel. I didn't know all this, I thought Judy was, as Ernie told me, "not well"—in fact, she had over-imbibed at lunch and was legless —while I was on stage, they were trying to sober her with black coffee.

On stage, I said to Jack Cuthcart, the musical director, "Give me an Al Jolson number." The band did a quick turnover to find the Mammy routine Mrs. Lastfogel had requested I should leave out. The audience cheered, it was the finish I was looking for. To her credit, she came backstage to my dressing room and said, "If I hadn't seen it with my own eyes, I'd never have believed it."

Walter Winchell was a columnist whose writing was syndicated throughout the United States. At an earlier age he had been a not too successful vaudeville performer, his voice was known to millions and there were many people in show business that would have given *anything* for a mention in his column, Judy included. If you saw the television series *The Untouchables*, you would know the staccato delivery on the soundtrack; it belonged to Winchell who would sit at a table in Lindy's restaurant throughout the evening while his minions scouted around New York for tasty morsels to fill his column.

He came to the show one evening and Judy introduced him to the packed audience. The patrons in the circle could not see him take a bow below in the stalls, so Judy encouraged him to come on stage. He was greeted with loud applause. She stopped her act to chat to him about show business, how he had once played the Palace as a turn and what did he do, "I did a buck and wing, Judy." She said. "Could you do it for us now?" Encouraged by the audience applause, he asked for a "stop" chorus of "Bye bye Blues"; he then went into a soft-shoe shuffle with the buck and wing finish—the audience went wild, they cheered him all the way back to his seat. Judy was clapping loudest.

Three nights later, Winchell was in again. Judy introduced him because, after his performance, he dedicated his whole column to her. This time they chatted longer—again he stopped the show. It was noticeable that poor Judy was finding it difficult to get going again. Lo and behold, a few nights later he came *again* and, as previously, always with half a dozen friends. Slowly it was turning into the Walter Winchell Show—each appearance his "spot" grew longer.

"How the hell do we get rid of this guy?" asked Judy after his fourth appearance. Sid Luft, Judy's manager, solved the problem—he whispered to Winchell that members of the Musicians' Union were not actually allowed to play for performers that were not on the bill and under contract. It was a bit of flannel but it worked and Winchell stayed away from then on, but Judy didn't get too many mentions after that.

Judy behaved for the rest of the run and gave no more worry to the stage crew, dancers and executives. I had to return to England after ten weeks, leaving a $2,500 a week job to appear in pantomime in Newcastle for £175 a week. I had signed a contract with Tom Arnold to play Buttons in *Cinderella*. I wasn't over the moon about this date because, no matter how much I closed my eyes, Newcastle just wasn't Broadway.

The good thing about the American engagement was that I was able to pay off the mortgage for the semi and, with a bigger family, think about a larger abode. I found the house that was perfect for us in Stanmore, still in north London.

In 1952, I had put quite a few more songs into my act; especially now I was making more records, audiences wanted to hear the songs I had made that were being played constantly on record programmes.

Into my life walked Bob Dixon, a pianist who hailed from Ulverston in Lancashire. He was standing on the corner of Denmark Street and Charing Cross Road; he had been playing dates with the Beverley Sisters but was working anywhere he could. He nodded, we chatted, he told me he had accompanied me in the pit orchestras on a couple of occasions. I said that I was now making quite a few broadcasts. He handed me a card with his telephone number and a request that if I ever needed a rehearsal piano player, to give him a call.

A week later, I called him. He came over to my house, sat down at the Bluthner I had recently purchased, then magic came from his fingers—it was warm, sweet and sympathetic to my style. At the time of writing, we have worked together for thirty-five years, travelled round the world twenty-three times, appeared on eighteen Royal Variety Shows and had a million laughs. He often tells people that if he had been standing on the other side of the road, he might have missed all this. *Bob likes a drink—but I think his eyesight is failing—he keeps running into pubs. He joined Alcoholics Anonymous—he still drinks but he does it under a different name. It was his birthday last week—I couldn't give him the present I would like to have given him—how do you gift wrap a brewery?*

11

MY parents were still living in the Buildings. I found them a new small three-bedroom house in Welling, Kent. They were delighted with it and they never had to worry about another thing financially until their dying day, which was not all that long ago.

By now, 1952, my four sisters had married, brother Harry had wed a pretty young girl named Jean Lewis, who was to make him a wonderful wife and present him with five sons, almost as quickly as my mother had given birth to us. Harry had gone back to stevedoring at the Surrey Commercial Docks. One night, he came to see me in my dressing room at the Palladium; he looked ghastly. He had hurt his back falling from a rigging, he was unable to sleep well and although a strong and healthy man, at this visit he looked poorly. It was that night I suggested he might get out of the docks and try something he had mentioned once or twice before, to be a publican. I told him that if he learned the trade, I would sponsor him. This he did and became one of the most successful landlords in south London. He kept me supplied with stories, most of them true, that his customers passed on, and there was always a welcome any time I walked in. Also he kept my mother supplied with her favourite tipple—Guinness. She once complained of swollen ankles; Harry said, "It's the sediment from the Guinness." *I now had a big house, a big car and a big head.*

When the pantomime run in Newcastle had closed, I received another telegram from America—Judy was to appear for six weeks at the Philharmonic Auditorium in Los Angeles and the William Morris Agency wanted me to appear with her. Jock upped the salary to $3,000, and this they agreed to.

I had never seen a palm tree growing before. When I arrived at the Hollywood Roosevelt Hotel, I just stared at those tall trees, telling me there were no winter nights here—not the sort of cold nights I was used to back home anyway.

I couldn't believe it either when I walked into the restaurant for lunch, and there sitting almost opposite was film star Gary Cooper with his wife. I watched him talking for forty-five minutes non-stop and wondered why in most of his films he just said, "Yep".

There are some performers who are filled with fear before they walk on a stage— Des O'Connor has confessed to me of times when he suffered stage fright that made him physically sick. Ronnie Barker is another who prefers to make a living as the good writer he is rather than tread the boards as a live entertainer. Me, I can't wait to walk on and show off—I love it— still do.

I once decided to take six months off; it was fatal—after three weeks, Blossom begged me to change my mind and take some engagements. For one thing, she didn't like me nosing around in her kitchen, interfering with the culinary chores—for another, Jock was missing the manager's fees he was used to collecting, and more, I really did miss the smell of the greasepaint.

Eric Morecambe once said, "When I open the fridge door and the light goes on, I finish up doing a ten-minute act to the frozen vegetables."

After a few nights at the Philharmonic Auditorium with Judy Garland, I received a fan letter from film actor James Mason. Not only was he most complimentary, he also invited me for Sunday lunch to his home on Rodeo Drive. I warned him that I had my three children and Blossom with me but he didn't mind. "Bring who you like," he said.

On the Sunday, Blossom and I arrived at Mason's Beverly Hills mansion with Anthony, Christine and Maxine, and Bob Dixon. We were greeted at the door by his wife Pamela Kellino, a lady with an electric personality, who made us so at home. We were ushered into the garden to meet faces we had only ever seen on the cinema screens. They were all charming, especially Frank Sinatra, who seemed to have a special affinity with solo stage performers, I suppose because he knew the challenge most of us face standing alone in a spotlight, trying to make hundreds of people applaud our efforts. *I used to be vain and swollen-headed—thought I was the greatest thing since canned beer—then I saw a psychiatrist—now I'm one of the most lovable men you ever met.*

Incidentally, when I went to the memorial service for James Mason at the small actors' church in Covent Garden two years ago, a batch of gossip writers from the dailies asked what my connection with the actor was, especially as the church was filled with some of the great names from English theatre. I seemed a little out of place among this "legitimate" throng.

I could have told them about that Sunday afternoon at his home in Hollywood when three of us, James, myself and Frank Sinatra, were standing by the poolside chatting. Suddenly, Mason's eyes opened wide, he pushed past us, then fully clothed jumped into the pool to rescue my five-year-old son, Anthony, who had his legs trapped in an inflatable lifebelt and was drowning. It shows how vain actors and performers are; there must have been thirty-odd people round the pool and only one of us noticed a little boy in difficulties. Mason did, and that incident sums him up

—he cared for others. We remained friends for the rest of his days. *I have taught all my children to swim just as my father taught me. Dad would take me to the end of the pier, drop me in, then I would have to swim back to land—that wasn't the hard part, the hard part was cutting my way out of the sack!*

From Los Angeles, we moved to the Curran Theatre in San Francisco. Judy had never missed a performance during the six-week run in LA. Mostly, because like many of us, she liked to show off to the Tinseltown élite. I cannot remember a show we did there when a big cinema star was not seated out in the audience somewhere—Bogart, Cary Grant, Lucille Ball, Alan Ladd, I could go on and on. San Francisco was a different story. Though situated in California, it is five hundred miles from the studios of Hollywood. Consequently, the audience that filled the place was Joe Public and Judy didn't spark unless she was impressing somebody "out front". She was bored with "Frisco."

The second Sunday we were there, she crossed the Golden Gate Bridge to

Berkeley for a quiet wedding ceremony to Sid Luft, her manager. Sid was a great friend to Bob Dixon and me, always ensuring we were happy and comfortable. Although a tough cookie, not averse to using a little strong-arm, he was never anything but a gentleman to my group. Sid was also a compulsive gambler.

Three days after the wedding, he told Judy he had to travel to Hollywood "on business". He was in the midst of producing a remake of *A Star is Born* with Judy as the star and James Mason playing the old Fredric March part.

When he hadn't returned by the Saturday, Judy blew her top. "On business? I know where the bastard is—he's at Saratoga race track—I'll get him back here double quick—cancel the matinée!"

The management begged and cajoled her to no avail—she was adamant. I had to go out on stage after my act to announce that "owing to the indisposition of our star, there would be no performance, money would be refunded or tickets for another show would be issued." There was great disappointment from the fans but Sid

174

was back on the next plane. That evening, they smooched like the honeymooners they, in fact, were.

After Judy had missed a couple of performances, people became wary of booking for the show and business began to drop off. It didn't help when a respected writer for the *San Francisco Examiner*, Herb Cain, made it known that the supporting cast of the show had gone to the Veterans Hospital and entertained the wounded back from Korea but Judy had begged off because of throat trouble —"Yet," Cain went on, "she found time to warble in a tavern at 2 o'clock the same morning . . ."

The publicity we were getting was bad —to stimulate interest, I was asked to go on a television chat show, mostly to assure the public that if they attended our show Judy *would* appear.

The TV show was a "plug" so any performer got only a token fee, twenty-five dollars, not a lot for half an hour of entertainment. I forget the name of the lady who interviewed me but we got round to talking about the differences between America and Great Britain.

I told her that what I noticed in cafés and bars was a degree of cleanliness that we didn't have in England, yet, I reminded her, if one went into one of these bars and unthinkingly put one's hands under the table, they felt large wads of chewing gum that people had taken from their mouths and stuck there—it made one want to get to the washroom quickly in case of contamination. She agreed it was a filthy habit. Next day, Herb Cain (who is still SF's favourite columnist) made a story of it with a headline that read, "Britisher Deplores Gum Habit". He had many letters sympathising with folks who disliked this dirty practice.

Several nights later, I arrived at the Curran to find two young executives in dark suits with crew haircuts, waiting for me. They explained they were from the advertising agency with a client who was one of the biggest manufacturers of chewing gum in the US and that my comments could do them irreparable harm —they suggested I go on the same programme, which they'd arrange, and explain that there is greaseproof wrapper to keep and then use for secondhand gum disposal—tell viewers this and it would help the cause. I mentioned the terrible fee the TV station were paying, they quadrupled it and before I left the programme, the lady interviewer gave me an old English sheepdog, "to take home to the children".

The dog was nine weeks old and already fairly big. I didn't want a dog—I was on tour, how could I look after it? Even if I did keep it, I could never get it back to England. Nobody in the studio would take it so I was left to walk it back to the St. Francis Hotel on Geary Street.

As soon as I walked in the foyer, the concierge came over. He knew me quite well by now, and politely he told me, "No pets". I phoned up to my room and asked Blossom to bring the kids down to the street and see what I had for them. Ten minutes later, they trooped down to see the new addition to the tour. The dog was so friendly, the children adored him. "What are you going to do with him?" asked Blossom. I didn't have an answer. "I'll take him to the theatre dressing room and figure out something," I told her.

That evening, I fed him with dog food

I bought at the supermarket; he lapped up a whole pint of milk, then repaid me by peeing all over the dressing room floor. I took him out on the street to see if he would do his big jobs near a tree—he didn't bother, then when he got back in the dressing room, he did the lot. I used a whole *San Francisco Examiner* to clear up his mess.

He yelped blue murder when I locked him in the room alone, there was no way I could leave him. I even tried running away from him but he galloped alongside me thinking it was all a great game. That night, to keep him quiet, I took him on stage with me. *What a good dog you are looking at—a wonderful house dog—we always know when burglars are near the house—he faints! I've had him since he was a puppy—he looked like two dirty mops tied together—we had him for three weeks before I found out I was talking to the wrong end—I got some very unusual answers.*

I slept that night with him in the dressing room. I wished there was some way I could keep him because we got on so well. I was saved the next day when one of the staff said, "Gee, what a swell dog —I'd give anything to own an old English sheepdog." I gave the dog to him, for which he thanked me—the kids cried for a week for giving him away. I heard from the man ten years later, who told me he had been a faithful and true friend, but now he had "left for that big ol' dog pound in the sky".

The show finished in San Francisco, we said goodbye to Judy and Sid. Jock Jacobsen, in the meantime, did something I was never too pleased with—he sold his business to MCA, the biggest agency in the US. He asked me if I would still let him handle me, as the agreement was for Jock to take his clients with him. He collected from Music Corporation of America for this and as he only had me as the main client, I became part of the furnishing at 135 Piccadilly for several years. I paid ten per cent of all earnings to them.

Before I left for England, MCA booked me into Las Vegas, almost unknown at the time. It was a strip with casinos that used acts to entertain the gambling crowds.

Today it is a city, then it was a street with a few neon lights, made possible to reside in by the installation of air-conditioning.

At Lake Tahoe in Nevada, I was booked to share the bill with a very attractive coloured singer named Dorothy Dandridge who had just starred in a blockbuster film *Carmen Jones*. The public were expecting the big operatic tones they had heard in the film, but that was a dubbed voice. Dorothy had a small nightclub singer's delivery and there was no way she could please them. She later committed suicide.

The club I worked at was owned by Nick and Harold Sahati, two Italians with alleged Mafia connections, they were brothers whose very looks commanded obedience. In those days, most acts were allotted fifteen minutes or so, but on one particular night with an exceptionally good audience, I did seven minutes over my time. After I had changed and washed off, I was walking through the restaurant on my way home when Nick Sahati stopped me. "Nice act tonight, kid," he said, without taking the cigar from his mouth. Pleased to be complimented by the boss, I thanked him. "In future, stick to your time—tonight you were twenty-two minutes—understand?" He turned and walked away.

One of the casino croupiers, whom I knew well, overheard this. I turned to him as Nick left. "What's eating the boss—I did all right with the crowd."

The croupier, a New Yorker, explained quietly what I had done wrong. "Look— you did seven minutes over. Seven days a week that comes to almost fifty minutes— you are here for three weeks—you have made two hours of gambling time vanish. It's sad, Mr. Englishman, but it's a business fact."

I never ran over time again—at least not at Sahati's.

12

APPEARING in pantomime is probably the toughest form of theatre there is. On my return from the States, I was booked to star at the Palladium as Buttons in *Cinderella*. My supporting cast was strong indeed, and although they hadn't then achieved the fame they are known by today, they were determined to be star names. Julie Andrews played Cinderella and Richard Hearne, who became a television personality as Mister Pastry.

As I said, pantomime is a tough game; bore the youngsters for too long and they'll begin to chatter or want to go to the loo, be too sophisticated, they'll yawn and kick their seats.

I love children (though I couldn't eat a whole one!) and towards the finale of the show, it was my job to "do the front cloth". This comes as they set the stairs, the lights, the ponies and the glittering walk down for the finish behind the front runners. I would be out frontleading the kids with "There's a tiny house . . ." a song where they repeat the line that I sang. This gave the stage-hands a good five minutes to set up for the last scene. I had to fill that five or six minutes and I did it with a most novel idea. The dialogue would go like this . . .

Buttons: Well, Cinderella has got her crystal slipper back—isn't it wonderful?
Kids: Yes, Buttons.
Buttons: Do you know something?
Kids: No-o-o-o, Buttons.
Buttons: We've lost the other one.
Kids: Ooh!
Buttons: Does anybody in the audience have it?
Kids: No, Buttons.
(Meanwhile an usherette would find a likely-looking infant and surreptitiously place the crystal slipper under their seat)
Buttons: Will you all look under your seat to see if it is there—

There would be a noise of a thousand or more tip-up seats all going together. Suddenly a cry: "Here it is, Buttons!" I would ask the finder to bring it to me on the stage. If they did I would give them a wonderful present. Providing the usherette had done her job properly, an angelic child would run down the aisle, mount the stage, the slipper in its little fist, then hand it over triumphantly and wait for the present.

First, I would do some time-wasting patter with the child, like asking them if they were married, name of teacher, where they lived, and so on. Then tell them that because they had found the crystal slipper, Prince Charming had sent them a special present. I'd clap my hands and immediately from the wings two flunkeys would appear with a brand-new silver bicycle on a large purple cushion. "By kind permission of Raleigh Cycles", who had a credit in the programme.

There were "oohs" and "aahs" at this, also a few screams and tears from other children in the audience who also wanted one. During one matinée, I had a devil of a job and almost a nasty accident as I prepared to give the bicycle to a little tyrant who gave me a real hard time. Where almost every other child trembled with excitement at the sight of the bicycle, this little punk just eyed it coolly, then said, "I've got one!" I whispered, "Well, take it home for your brother." His reply was, "I ain't got a brother, I'm an only child." For some reason, nothing would induce him to take it. I clowned around a little, hoping he'd decide to have it—then I had an idea.

"This bicycle is the strongest bicycle in the whole world," I told him and the audience. "Even I can ride it." The audience egged me on. "Go on then," they screamed. I am over six feet tall but managed to sit on the small machine and push the pedals, much to the amusement of the packed house. I rode round and round the stage as the audience laughed and applauded. Then, without warning, this little devil rushed forward and pushed me into the orchestra pit. A couple of the musicians saw me coming and broke the fall. The little horror, seeing what he'd done, tore down the stairs and into the auditorium, where his mother cuddled him and told him not to worry. I got away with bruises but later told the usherette, "No more boys—in future, make sure it's girls who find the slipper."

The following year I starred in *Mother Goose*, also with Richard Hearne and Peter Sellers. Peter was a most unhappy man during the run. His ambition was to get into making movies. He was having a fair amount of success with *The Goon Show* but it was a cult following at that time, so much so that a BBC executive, in all seriousness, referred to it as the "Go—on—Show".

Peter had created a very funny character named Major Bloodnok whom he decided to use as the Baron in the pantomime. Unfortunately, it did not travel across the floodlights, it was essentially a radio character. Each day he became more and more morose, especially when the finale came and Bloodnok walked down to mediocre applause. The family audience did not like the character. It was a shame because Peter had gone to great lengths to make Bloodnok real, he had padded his stomach, greyed his hair even though he was only in his late twenties, built his nose up with putty and spent careful time prodding the putty with a cherry stick, to give it the look of a pockmarked hooter, which he reddened with carmine. It did not work. Daily he became more disenchanted with his role; what kept him going was the fact he was being paid more than he had ever earned before.

There is a scene in *Mother Goose*, played in this instance by Richard Hearne, where she has so much wealth she sells her soul to become beautiful. When this old crone comes out of the fountain in a gold lamé dress and wig studded with diamonds, it was Peter's entrance to rush on stage, see her and exclaim, "My God, what is this?" One particular performance, he decided to change the character; instead of entering as Bloodnok, he changed the make-up to that of Groucho Marx with cigar and stooped walk. He advanced towards Mother Goose and instead of giving the line, "My God, what is this?," he changed it to a life-like impression of Groucho and said, "I've heard of Lady *Dicker* but this is *ridoculous*". The fellows in the orchestra howled with laughter but Richard Hearne, who had spent most of his time in legitimate theatre, would not utter the next line until Peter had given him the proper cue—there was a silence and stage wait that seemed like an eternity.

The next day, I walked into Peter's dressing room; he sat there with a letter in his hand, tears rolling down his cheek. I thought a near relative had passed away. When I asked him if there was anything wrong, he handed me the letter and asked me to read it. It had been sent from Moss Empires head office and delivered by hand, and was signed by the big white chief, Val Parnell. I can remember it almost word for word . . .

Dear Mr. Sellers:

I was in the theatre yesterday when you decided to change the text of Mother Goose.

When I require you to make the members of my orchestra laugh, I will ask you.

Until then, do the job you are being paid for, otherwise I will have you personally kicked out of the theatre.

Yours, etc
Val Parnell

When the pantomine run was over, I was to have the starring part in a major movie to me made at Shepperton called *Charlie Moon*, and there was a part in it heaven-made for Peter. Sellers begged me to talk to the producers in the hope they would use him. I did. I told Colin Leslie, the producer, that Peter was a huge talent, but they had seen him in the *Mother Goose* show, were not impressed and gave the part to Michael Medwin. Luckily, the Boulting Brothers saw his potential, put him into some of their early films and Peter gained the glory that his talent richly deserved.

Working at the Palladium so often gave me a great chance to enjoy my home, Blossom and my three children. We are a close family and loved doing things together. The producers liked the idea of Anthony playing me as an eight-year-old in *Charlie Moon*; it worked very well too. We had many days on location down in Hampshire together.

If I was booked for a summer show at one of the resorts, I would rent a house for the family. That way we didn't have to spend months apart. It was while we were all at Torquay in Devon, the following happened. I was asked to take some of the artistes on the bill and perform a show for prisoners in Dartmoor Prison, some twenty miles away. I liked appearing in prison concerts; I had done concerts at Wormwood Scrubs and the ladies' prison, Holloway—I liked it because as I informed the inmates. "You are a captive audience." *Roll on the drum, Ray!*

The joke I invariably opened with was, "Chilly in here—could somebody run down and close the front gates." *Hit the cymbal, Ray.*

Once you are through those forbidding studded doors of Dartmoor Prison, there is a pleasant surprise waiting if you are not an inmate. Inside are beautiful lawns and shrubs, tended lovingly by some of the most hardened criminals imaginable. The doors around are painted in bright colours, the whole atmosphere reminds one of an old-fashioned Butlin's Holiday Camp, only the warders unlocking and relocking the doors makes one aware that Butlin's it isn't.

The prisoners on concert days are

dressed in neat battle-dress-type uniforms, not unlike RAF blue. They wear collars with ties, some of them laugh and joke with you.

Five years previously, while working at the Palace Theatre in Manchester, my dressing room had been burgled. One item stolen was a lighter presented to me by the St. Anne's Youth Club in Vauxhall. I was appearing at the time in *Jack and the Beanstalk*. A week or two after the robbery, on my way into the Midland Hotel, a dark figure stepped from the shadows; he said, "Excuse me—do you recognise this?" He held the stolen lighter for me to inspect. I asked him how he had got it and he told me he had bought it from a fellow in a pub for two pounds. If I would like to give him the two quid he had paid out for it, I could have it back. I felt in my pocket for two pounds, gave it to him, and he then disappeared. As I walked into the light of the hotel clutching the lighter and pound notes, I didn't know whether to smile or not: as Jack in the show I became rich—the money we used was stage money, not unlike the green pound notes in circulation, except that printed across the back of our notes was "All that glitters is not gold". Sometimes I would forget and stuff them in my going-home clothes.

After the concert at Dartmoor, we were taken to the Governor's office and given tea with home-made cakes with Devon cream. The trustee serving us was a face vaguely familiar; he asked for permission to speak, which was granted. He told the story about this stage actor who had worked him two counterfeit notes years before in Manchester, adding as he pointed to me, "He's a con man—he should be in here, not me, sir." Amid great laughter, I had to tell the Governor it was absolutely true.

Our house in Edgware was a large one with eight bedrooms, a billiard room, a tennis court and through the back garden gate was a five-acre lake. We encouraged our children to bring their friends home. In summer they would swim or fish in the large lake, in winter there was a heated summer-house, where games and chats took place. They had bicycles, scooters and most things but, at the same time, we tried to keep them level-headed. They went to good schools and Blossom behaved like a mother hen. Her one goal was to keep a warm loving home for her children and keep me happy, which she did admirably.

At that time, the competition for her was totally unfair. Invariably the shows I appeared in had anything from a dozen to twenty fabulous-looking dancing girls, the places I was eating in had, in many instances, the world's greatest chefs. If I came back from an interview and happened to say I had enjoyed a meal at the Savoy or the Café Royal, she would ask me what I had to eat. Without saying anything, she would look up one of her numerous cookbooks and, sure enough, it would be on the table a week later. She would watch my reaction to see if the food compared well with the Dorchester, and many times it was better. She still makes chicken soup better than any restaurant I know. Omelettes are the fluffiest, also she cooks pork chops to her own recipe. So, competing with the glamour and the gourmet cooks she was, and still is, doing a great job. If I did a joke routine about her cooking, she would forgive—she knew that if I stopped making the customers laugh, we might finish up back at Plumstead Common in two rooms. *You should see her rhubarb pie—one inch wide and two feet long—what's more, she's colour blind—it was celery.*

Sometimes I am asked if she objects to a particular joke—she never does, in many cases she finds ways to improve a routine. The following got big laughs and much of it came from adding bits she thought of . . .

A few weeks ago, my wife said, "Max"— she's got a wonderful memory for names. She said, "Max, I think I'll get a new dress." I said, "What's wrong with the last one I bought you?" She said, "Nothing, but when I go shopping in it—people throw confetti."

We have little arguments—sometimes she wins—sometimes I win—in this case she lost—which was a pity 'cos she had lovely teeth.

She went to the sales the other day, came back full of joy. "I bought an eider-

194

down, a pair of sheets and a hovercraft,"
she said. "I'm going out in it tomorrow."
Honestly—three thousand miles of open
sea and she backs into the Isle of
Wight . . .

It was a long routine; it may not look it in
cold print but the laughs came thick and
fast. Blossom often says, "You did well
for a seven and sixpenny marriage licence,
didn't you? Mother, housekeeper and
scriptwriter."

About that time, I had written the
words and music for a song called, "You
Need Hands"; it was a very big hit both
here and in the USA. When I sang it to
her, she said, "Speaking of hands—we
could do with a few pairs of those around
here." Up till then, she had tried to do
the lot, not because she was some sort of
Amazon, but because she didn't believe
the help we had had in the past came up
to her standards. I went to Ireland with
her and interviewed about twenty girls
in Belfast. We decided on two lovely
young ladies, Kathy and Evelyn; they
were sisters, and both of them stayed with
us for many years. I also got myself a

chauffeur/handyman named Tom, who also stayed for a long time until he emigrated to join his mother in Australia. With all these, as well as the gardener, the house was always full of people—it was cheerful, happy, and life was very sweet. That's how the Fifties were for us.

There wasn't too much outdoor entertainment being filmed at that time, so with cameras, crew, make-up and lighting technicians, we went into the Sixties with a show called *"Roamin' Holiday"*. Eric Sykes helped with the scripts. On the Italian Riviera, we set about making one of the first overseas series ever seen on British television.

We were one big happy family.

13

ALASSIO is the holidaymakers' dream, cool Mediterranean breezes, golden sands, friendly people, with a way of life that allows for a little shut-eye in the afternoon, then long nights for living it up. I feel that when I was born, it was in the wrong country, I would have made an acceptable Italian in every way. The food is to my liking, the climate is everything I desire, the language is rhythmic and easy to learn. When we discovered it in the early Fifties, it became our annual treat for all the family and they loved it.

Now, unfortunately, the motorway passes overhead so there are not so many vacationers dropping off. I recollect with affection the days and nights spent there.

Jack Soldani owned a small café near the main square, it was Jack who taught me to "fish trout" with "cherries". Jack, a big man, with a Groucho Marx moustache and humour to match, would drop everything to go into the mountains with his rod and line. I tested him once on this: he was serving coffee to a Swedish couple who were quite demanding. He had to go back into the kitchen for extra hot water, go again for cream, *not* milk, they asked for extra napkins. I could see Jack was getting uptight with the demands so I said, "Fancy going up in the mountains for some fish, Jack?"

Before I had finished the question, he had his apron off, given it to his twelve-year-old daughter behind the cash desk, and with a "ritorno subito—ciao", the two of us climbed into his little Fiat and were heading for the mountains before you could say "Sophia Loren".

Beside a stream, we tackled up and set about catching the trout that Jack would sell later that evening in his café. At first, I thought he was having me on about the cherries—but no. At a bend in the stream hung the branches of a cherry tree; through the years, as the cherries ripened and fell into the stream, the trout became accustomed to eating them. All it needed was a float plus a medium-size hook, then "strike". It was rare for us to leave with fewer than half a dozen good-sized fish.

As we sat on the bank, Jack would tell me of his exploits in the Italian army, of Mussolini, of wartime Alassio. One story that stays in my mind was about the piano. In the centre of town, the Germans had commandeered the largest hotel for headquarters. They helped themselves to anything they liked. One of their likes was a Steinway piano they confiscated from a house belonging to some English people who had fled back to Britain when war was declared. When the conflict was over, the English couple returned to their home in Alassio but, of course, most of their beautiful furniture had been ruined by the Germans. The piano had vanished and although extensive inquiries were made it could not be found. They purchased another piano and had the same blind piano-tuner they had employed before the war to call and look after its tuning.

One day, there was a loud banging on their door; they opened it to find the piano-tuner in his dark glasses with his white stick unable to contain himself. "Your Steinway is in Alassio!" he blurted.

They asked him where but he could not tell them, all he could say was that he was walking through one of the small alleys near the Café Roma when he heard it being played. When they argued that it might not have been theirs, he was adamant. "I serviced your piano for twelve years before the war—I know the strings, the pads, the pedals—I know wherever that piano is—it is the one I tuned every month for twelve years."

They followed the tuner to the spot. For days they waited to hear it being played. One day, to the strains of "Leibestraum", they traced the apartment and the player. They knocked at the door and waited. The playing ceased, the door was opened by a dark-eyed little grey-haired old lady. She heard the story, then invited them in to inspect the piano. It *was* the one that belonged to the English couple. They assumed there would be a long legal battle to prove ownership, but the old lady waved her hands and said, "Take it, tomorrow two young lads were taking it away to a tip up the mountainside, it will save me 3000 lire."

As far as I know, that Steinway, which

today would cost more than £5,000, is still there.

The Café Roma is owned by three hard-working brothers, one of whom is named Mario, lovely rotundo, smiling Mario—he is a fine painter who has exhibited in London, Rome, Monte Carlo and various other capitals. I have several of his paintings, some I bought, others he has given to me, they hang in my home and are admired. A friend of Picasso's, with several of the great man's works that Pablo presented to him as gifts, he spoke no English but we always got by. He and his brothers, Georgio and Tomasso, worked all the hours that God sent. At three in the morning, Tomasso would go home to his beautiful wife and baby, Georgio would lock up then go "trolling" for signorinas who were on vacation—he liked the English variety. Mario would go to his lovely family who lived in the windmill he had converted to a unique home, and there he would paint for a few hours before turning in.

Imagine the jolt I got one morning in England to open the newspaper and read that an Italian painter in Italy had been kidnapped and a large ransom demanded for his return. The painter was none other than my friend Mario.

Telephone lines to small villages in countries like Italy left a lot to be desired but when I eventually got through, I learned that Mario had vanished into thin air; the family didn't want to say much as one of the demands of the kidnappers was —no publicity. When the ransom was paid, the brothers were left almost penniless. They had to start all over again, but with that Italian tenacity, they did. I keep meaning to drop in on them and I know that when I do, and I will, the three of them will take things up exactly where we left off. I loved Alassio, and when I talked Lew Grade's television company into making a series of films from there, it made the place famous. The following year, three-quarters of a million more visitors came; the next year, we couldn't find a house even to rent—in the meantime, I had been made honorary mayor! A mayor with no parlour.

The filming of *Roamin' Holiday* was completed, we returned to England, suntanned, happy and rested—unaware that from these bright happy carefree days, many dark hours were to emerge. The record business had been extremely good to me during the Fifties, songs that were to become standards had reached the Top Ten, time and time again: "Tulips From Amsterdam", "Mr. Sandman", "Heart of My Heart", "You Need Hands", "Davy Crockett", "Friends and Neighbours", were just a few. I kicked off the Sixties with a winner, "Fings Ain't Wot They Used T'Be", but the music scene was changing rapidly. The record-buying public was getting younger, and they liked artistes their own age: Cliff Richard, Tommy Steele and soon The Beatles, were pushing aside names like mine, Frankie Vaughan, and David Whitfield. After "Fings" it would be another eight years before I got back into the charts. It didn't worry me all that much because I had a full date-book for theatres up and down the country, also I was regularly flying to and from New York appearing on television shows that included the Ed Sullivan Show, the Perry Como Show, Bob

Crosby and guest appearances with Jack Benny.

We had finished filming *Roamin' Holiday* in Alassio. During that stint, my daughter Christine, now an attractive seventeen year old, met and became engaged to Michael Richards, who was the floor manager of the TV series. Mike was just three years older than Christine and I liked him a lot. Soon after her eighteenth birthday, she informed us that she wanted to marry Mike. I tried to tell them they were too young but they laughed and pointed at Blossom and me, saying, "How can you talk, married with children when you were not much older."

There was nothing we could do to dissuade them, so, one very wet Sunday, at the little Catholic church in Edgware, Christine became Mrs. Richards. The reception was held at a restaurant I part-owned in Stanmore. Many of my great friends from show business came, the Harry Secombes, the Eric Sykeses, the Cliff Michelmores, Alma Cogan, Joan Regan and many more, one hundred and twenty guests altogether. The couple were deliriously happy at their own little house in Barnet and almost three months later, Christine told us we were to become grandparents—we were both thirty-eight. I can't remember whether we were shocked with joy or sadness at the thought; however, we dressed up, got in the car, drove up to the Berkeley Hotel off Piccadilly and did the Twist to Chubby Checker until 3 a.m.

Blossom had always thought that many houses were planned wrong; architects seemed to be men who rarely took the needs of women into consideration. For ages she had sat with pencil and sketch board, dreaming up what she considered to be the perfect home. By now, I was comparatively wealthy so, on the spur of the moment one day, I suggested we look for some land to build on. We found three acres in the middle of Leatherhead Golf Course, it cost £9,500 and had belonged to Charlie Smirke, top jockey of the Forties and Fifties. After we bought the land I went to the RIBA in Portland Place and asked them to suggest an architect to carry out Blossom's scheme; they recommended

Mr. Cantacazino, a very competent man.

Nine months later, the house was completed, with five bedrooms, five bathrooms, billiard room, a lounge that extended, dining room with room-divider for sitting room, a dream kitchen and utility room. Around the L-shaped house on the first floor was a walkway that led across a bridge to the garage, staff quarters and spireshaped roof that was a playroom. At the top of the spire, Blossom put a Dutch windmill weathervane that we would curtsy to each morning because I put the story about that the house had been built from the royalties of "Tulips From Amsterdam".

All the materials were of the highest quality, from the black shiny tiles on the roof and the teak wood throughout, to the underfloor heating. We stinted on nothing, yet for all this, including the landscaped gardens, the entire project came to less than £70,000. To build the same today would cost more than ten times that. We called it Pentice Walk and we loved it there. The dogs ran freely, I bought a small motor mower with which to cut the lawn, Old Bert tended the flowerbeds while Anthony practised playing his drums up in the playroom, which was pretty soundproof.

One Sunday, I was asked to play in a Pro-Am tournament at Leatherhead Golf Club. There were many well-known personalities playing. It suited me because my house was on the course so there was no travelling to be done. All I needed was my studded shoes, which I took to the locker-room to change. I was appearing at the Palladium at the time and on the night previously, I had had a mishap. I made my entrance on a horse, a big wonderful creature called Goldie. He was a circus horse, trained by Vera Cody. By touching him in different places and giving him different words of command, he would bring the place down with applause. When I dismounted, I would bring him to the front of the stage and ask him questions; then, by tickling him in the right spot and rewarding him with a few lumps of sugar, he would appear to the audience to be talking back to me. Actually, what happened was an off-stage microphone was used, with a man who would fake the voice of Goldie. After the chat, I would mount again, the band would play "Tea for Two Cha-Cha", Goldie would swing his bottom in time to the music—exit to tumultuous applause.

The night before the golf tournament, Goldie had trodden on my toe—I wore soft shoes and the pain was excruciating. What's more he didn't move, once he was on my foot—unless you've had a ton of horsemeat on your toes, you won't appreciate how painful it can be. Now it was the morning after. I was in the locker room inspecting my bruised toes when one of the players walked up behind me and said, "Hello old boy, how are you?"

Without looking up, I said, "Not so good—I've got a bad toe—I'm just wondering if I can get round eighteen holes."

He snorted, said, "Bloody sorry about you, old chap," then he walked off, clanking as he went. I still shudder with embarrassment each time I think of it. The man I had been complaining to was Douglas Bader, the legless pilot, hero of the Second World War, the man who had known more pain with his lost legs than almost any man living, yet here I was beefing about a couple of bruised toes—I made a vow never to complain about my lot again—I don't know whether I have stuck to it but I meant to.

14

CHRISTINE and Mike had a beautiful girl they named Louise. They came to Leatherhead to stay with us for the birth. Blossom was in high gear acting as midwife and enjoying every moment. When Christine took Louise back to her own place, it left a big void in the house as all things revolved around the baby; we all missed her when she'd gone but looked forward to the visits. Not long after she left, the phone rang at seven one Sunday morning; it was Christine. I didn't know what she would be calling for at that hour, and she was crying. I asked her what was wrong; she said, "Mike's had an accident."

"Is he hurt?" I asked. She choked back the tears. "He's dead—Daddy, what can I do?"

The police had knocked at her door an hour previously to tell her that Mike had given actor Ray Barrett a lift home from the studio because Ray's car would not start. After he'd dropped him, Mike had misread the road curve and gone into a tree. The Mini he was driving stood no chance and Mike was killed instantly.

I dressed as fast as I could, then drove to Barnet on the other side of London in record time. When I walked into the living room, the scene which met me would stay with me for ever. Christine, with her big red eyes, sat by the table nursing baby Louise, the table laid for one with a note she had left for Mike; it said,

"Very tired—going to bed—enjoy your dinner. XX Love you".

Christine came back to live with us at Pentice Walk. Then her friend and doctor, Keith Anderson, informed her that she was pregnant. Six months later, she gave birth to a son whom she named Michael John. The John was in memory of Mike's father who, shortly after the shock of his son dying, had a heart attack and passed away too. It was grey days for all of us. Almost everything around reminded us of the happy days now past. So when Jock came through with an offer to appear in

Australia for ten weeks, I took it and arranged to take my children, Blossom, Christine and the two babies, also the nanny Kathy, and Bob Dixon my pianist. The eight of us left for Melbourne in July 1963, the very place we had thought of emigrating to back in 1946.

Nowadays, through television, we have many films that acquaint us with the Australian way of life, twenty-six years ago I wasn't at all sure what it was about. *I was told that all the women dress the same —brown woolly dresses with a big pocket in front—they said, "Don't try to kiss 'em, they jump a mile"—they have Christmas dinner on the beach—roast octopus—it's not as nice as turkey but everybody gets a leg! Boom—boom.*

I wasn't prepared for Melbourne. The most vivid memory of that time was what they called "the six o'clock swill". The Australian workers would rush from the factory as the five o'clock whistle sounded, straight into the pub for a thirst slake before the barmaid shouted "Time!" At six o'clock sharp, it was "service over". The "midies" and "sevens" would be swilled down as fast as the barmaid could serve them and many left the bars legless.

There were a few fair restaurants, mostly in the St. Kilda area. Apart from that, most cafés served steak and chips or fish and chips. Over the years, the change is dramatic. In the old days, a comedian would need permission to say "damn" or "bloody", now many make an Eddie Murphy movie sound like Snow White. Restaurants are now as good as any in the world. I have been to Australia every year, apart from four years, since 1963. Recently there, I switched on a programme on ABC, which is equivalent to our BBC, and considered the good taste network. I couldn't believe what I was seeing. A comedy programme for the young with the title *Blah Blah Blah*, had a youthful compère putting a condom on a cucumber —absolutely true. *My wife walked into the room in the middle of it—she thought it was a cookery lesson—she sat with pencil and pad, waiting for the recipe—she said, "We'll have to get some of those." I said, "What—cucumbers?" She said, "No— condoms—we've never had courgettes in a bag!"*

In this year, 1988, it is possible, as a visitor, to see the changes. I was invited to a party in Rose Bay, Sydney, given by an old Australian actor named Chips Rafferty. In the early Sixties he was probably one of Australia's best known film stars. He sat on a wooden box swilling beer from a bottle. Blossom came up to ask me something from the other side of the room and he said, "You've crossed the line, darling." She asked what he meant, and he told her this was the men's end of the room and to get back to the other side with the womenfolk. It was as parochial as that in days gone by.

Then, fair dinkum Aussies were hard to find and most of the customers who came to the Tivoli to see me were expatriates who remembered me from *Educating Archie*, or seeing me at the Palladium or their provincial theatres; some had brought their recordings with them. Now it is different. Then, ninety per cent of our audiences were British, now it is the other way round, ninety per cent are Aussies. I enjoy them, I like their humour, their wit and their pride, I get along with them and admire the way they are trying to get their country to shape up to being their own, not influenced by the British way of life they have been compelled to follow for the past two hundred years.

When the dates in Australia were completed, I had to return to London because I had agreed to make another movie, called, *A Cry From the Streets*. Imagine our surprise when Christine told Blossom that she intended to stay in Melbourne with the children for a while. She thought that since losing Michael, there were too many memories back in the UK. She had worked previously as a beautician for Elizabeth Arden in Bond Street. Without letting us know, she had written to Myers, a large department store in Melbourne, for a job doing the same sort of thing. She got the job and reckoned she could cope with some help to look after the little ones during the day. We tried to talk her out of it, but all three of my children have always tried to stand on their own feet; they have never asked me for a penny, they are all fairly successful and their pride at being individuals makes me aware that once they've made up their minds—that's it—don't argue. I have looked after them in my own way but, as I say, never once can I remember their asking for a hand-out.

Reluctantly, we left Australia for the return to England. I watched Christine and the children waving from the barrier, Maxine sobbed and Blossom dried her tears, I heard "Bye Daddy" above the noise of aircraft taking off; my heart was heavy as lead, we were leaving our first child, a widow, on the Australian continent, alone, to make a new life.

The script for *Cry From the Streets* was a good one. The film was to receive many awards, the New York Critics Award of the Month—top film shown at the Edinburgh Festival—later, the Moscow Film Festival bought it—the only English-speaking film to be purchased. The director was a Londoner who knew the film game backwards; his name, Lewis Gilbert. I had made movies previously and I realised that few of the directors knew how to get the best from an actor. Most of them accepted what you did with lines you had learned the night before, but

Lewis was different. Because a film, for economic reasons, is shot disjointedly, it isn't always easy to remember how you approach the next scene. Lewis would rectify that, he'd say something like, "Back in scene ninety-two that we shot three week ago—remember—you entered from the street—that's as far as we got— the scene the cinema public will see in the next seconds is you entering the room bewildered—you take in the room—see the arm dangling from the bed—all the happiness leaves your face. Walk towards the arm, slowly, pick it up—hold it as though hoping to feel a pulse—let the arm fall—then I will call, Cut!"

Now, with instructions like that, you'd have to be pretty dumb not to turn in a good job. With Barbara Murray as leading lady and some great names of the British cinema in support, no wonder it was a good film, even though the budget was a tight one.

When Lewis was casting the film, which was a story of children from wrecked homes who end up in orphanages, he asked me to come with him to see what we could find on the streets around Kings

Cross and Islington, two London areas that had suffered badly in the Blitz. Lewis hoped to find some "naturals"—not the people who go to theatrical schools who all sound the same. The two of us pulled up in Lewis's car outside a block of flats in Kings Cross, very similar to the ones where I had started life at 7, Rye Buildings. About sixteen kids were playing a game of football with a tennis ball and the noise was deafening. Up on the landings were lines of washing, leaning on railings were mothers watching their broods enjoying themselves.

Lewis and I walked into this mêlée; his face was bright as he pointed to each one saying, "Look at that—look at the eyes on that one—look at those legs . . ." By now, some of the mothers, seeing strange men talking to their children, came down to investigate. Some of them recognised me and their concern turned to welcome. Lewis explained we were looking for about twenty children to take part in a film being made at Twickenham and we would return the following day to make the selection. The scruffy, unwashed group shouted things like "Don't forget me mister,"

"Will I do?", "I've always wanted to be a film star," and so on.

The next day, we saw a transformation. The kids who the day before could have graced a Dead End Kids movie were unrecognisable. They had been washed, hair shampooed, the boys wore little bow ties with hair greased down, the girls were in party dresses with bows in their hair—not a bit how Lewis imagined them for his picture. The mothers smiled at them from the sideline, all were on their best behaviour—it was awful. Luckily Lewis remembered them the way he had seen them the day before and booked the lot. The summer holidays were on so each morning a coach went to the Buildings to pick them up and drop them at locations, or the studios at Twickenham.

A few days into the filming, Lewis realised he had a bundle of charm in a four-year-old boy named David Bushell. He was constantly going in for close-ups on him. In one scene, Lewis suggested I sat him on my knee to tell him a story; it was Friday afternoon and, as often happens on film sets, technical faults with the camera developed. A "wrap" was called, we were told we would pick up the scene when we returned for shooting on Monday. With the weekend over, we returned to resume the scene we had left unfinished. When young David Bushell walked in there was a gasp—on the Sunday he had taken a pair of scissors and quietly cut off most of his hair. There was a panic call to the make-up department to make a wig exactly like David's own hair had looked before the scene we were about to shoot. When the wig was finished and David had cost the producers several hundred pounds in "hold-up" time, they tried to put the wig on him. We bribed him with Milky Ways and Smarties but he didn't want to know about a toupée that was held on with hair clips. We would get half-way through a "take", then he'd rip it off with a loud "I don't like it!", as he remembered the thatch on his head. The cameras had to stop as we tried to figure out what to do. The production staff stood around suggesting ways and means of making the scene work.

The problem was solved by a little girl of about seven—one of the kids on the Kings Cross coach; she said, "Smack his arse." David was in earshot when this was said and Lewis saw his eyes flicker for a moment. He said, "That's a good idea—get me a cane." David rushed back on the set to sit on my knee, Lewis stood behind the camera with the cane ready to shout "Action!" We got the scene in the very next "take", after twenty-three shots at it before. I don't know where David is now, he must be a mature man but wherever he is, I'd like him to know I've had many happy memories from that movie.

Another incident that gets my memory working, that happens on the odd occasions I have seen *A Cry From the Streets* on television, concerned a teenager named Jimmy. Jimmy isn't his real name but I'll call him that because he is happily married with a very good job in journalism, and we still see each other and are good pals. I asked him if he'd mind my relating this story—he said it was okay. So alive and bright was Jimmy at fifteen, he became chaperon and supervisor to all the children on the coach, organising their meals, taking them to the loo and also

221

playing the part of a trouble-maker in the film, which he did competently.

When the movie was completed and he asked me if there was a chance of a job, I suggested to Jock Jacobsen that he would be good for running messages, or answering the phone at our office. We gave him the job and he was excellent, always clean and tidy, always on time. When he answered phone inquiries, his very, very Cockney delivery vanished to become quite cultured: "Just one moment please —I'll see if Mr. Bygraves is available."

One Monday morning when he entered my office with the mail, his cheery, "Good morning sir" was dull—it made me look up. I sensed he was hiding his face from me. "Jimmy—let me look at your face." He slowly turned to show me his face that was beginning to fester, there wasn't a square inch of skin that hadn't been clawed and scratched.

"What happened?" I asked. He told me that playing football in the park the day before, he had run for the ball, couldn't stop and went headlong into some barbed wire. I wished him better and went on reading the mail. I couldn't concentrate,

222

then thought to myself it was unusual for barbed wire to be put anywhere near a football field. I called him on the buzzer. I said, "Jimmy, you are not telling me the truth—who did that to your face?" He stood there, head hung low. "Who did it Jimmy?" I repeated. Large teardrops fell on the carpet as he began to weep; he murmured something I couldn't hear. "Who?" I said. He sniffed the tears back, then said "My mother."

My office was just at the back of Leicester Square, a minute or two away from the offices of the Royal Society for the Prevention of Cruelty to Children—I walked him over there. He was reluctant to accompany me. When the gentleman at the office saw him, he "tut-tutted" and said he would investigate. The report came through that Jimmy was very demanding at home. On the Sunday, he waited for his mother to leave the pub to give him his "dinner" so he could go off to football. When she arrived home full the of spirit, a row developed, the result was that his mother, with this fiery Scotch background, tore into him and did the damage we could see.

When she saw what she had done to her son and he saw what he had done to her —they both reformed. She swore off the drink—he stopped antagonising and they lived happily ever after. He has never touched alcohol and does an enormous amount of work for charity; he even talked me into giving up a Saturday afternoon's football to go to Kings Cross Salvation Army and entertain a roomful of derelicts he had gathered.

Jimmy is one of my favourite people. I only tell the story because *Cry From the Streets* touched my life in so many ways, with so many incidents, I'm reluctant to mention them all at the risk of becoming maudlin.

15

TO some, the thought of travelling the world, stopping on the way at luxury hotels, is a lifelong dream; it was to me, but after the first half-dozen times it becomes as inspiring as a week's holiday in Sheffield. Remembering my humble background should have made me less blasé, but the thought of late nights arriving back at even some of the world's number one hotels, with dining rooms closed and, in those days, room service over at 10 p.m., makes one long for home life. Yet, it has to be done if one expects to have the pleasures the financial side of it brings.

The trick is to relieve the boredom; this can be achieved by learning to play golf, which I did, and am still learning—to write, books or essays, which I did and am still learning, or to play games, which I usually do when the other two aren't possible.

There is nothing worse than a four or

five-day stay in a hotel room, which you leave at 9.30 a.m.—hang the card on the doorknob that says, "Maid please tidy room", then returning at 1 p.m. after trying to pass the morning shopping with an umbrella that has blown inside out, to find the room hasn't been touched.

You then phone the housekeeper to tell her that although you put the notice out at nine-thirty and the maid has had three and a half hours to get round to it, the beds are not made, the towels are not changed, and so on. You remind them you are paying £100 a night, then they, full of apologies, tell you it will be attended to right away. You now go down into the lounge and try to kill another hour while the maid, who by now, dislikes you intensely because she has had a rocket from the housekeeper, makes the room up; in the meantime you think up "games".

Only a couple of years ago, the manager of a hotel in Melbourne, Australia, greeted me at the door. In the course of our conversation he told me that three weeks before, Eric Sykes had stayed there. He was a popular figure and kept the staff chuckling all the time. A little later on, I went to the Reception and asked for a few sheets of hotel headed notepaper. I then went up to my room and typed, with one finger, the following to Eric at his office in London:

Dear Mr. Sykes:
    On January 28th last, you left without paying your telephone account, this came to A$2347–63 (Two thousand three hundred and forty seven dollars, sixty three cents).
    We are sure this is an oversight on your part and will be glad to receive your cheque in settlement.
                        Yours, etc
                        Joseph King (Manager)

Eric was unaware that I was in Australia at the time, otherwise he would have suspected a ruse, especially as I had used a signature that was easy to rumble—Joseph King—becomes "Joe King" and Joe King becomes "joking", but for some reason it did not register with him.
    Three weeks later, I was having lunch with Eric at our favourite restaurant in London, when suddenly he talked about

227

the bill he had received from Australia. Realising that he didn't suspect me of sending the account, I played it up more. "Gosh—your name is mud in Melbourne—just before I left, I saw headlines that said, 'Eric Sykes ducks out of Oz leaving phone bill'." He stopped eating his spaghetti bolognese and said, "But I never spent more than five minutes on a phone in my life." He then came up with a theory that got me worried; he said "There was an Italian chambermaid on my floor—I'll bet she was phoning her family in Sicily from my room. I'll get in touch with the manager and tell him to investigate the chambermaid—trace the calls, I'll bet you she is the one that ran up the bill."

Oh dear, what a dilemma; first of all there was no Joseph King to call—if, when he called, he somehow got through to the manager, Eric would blow his top, then get the innocent chambermaid into trouble—I had to think of something. My secretary and right arm, Jennifer Maffini, speaks fluent Italian and manages a very good broken English-Italian too. Several days later, I told Jennifer to phone Eric saying she was calling from Sicily, that she was the

With Blossom, Maxine, Anthony, baby Ashley and little Lily. Anthony had three children under the age of three, I told him I'd take him to the zoo – let the rabbits have a look at *him!*

With Cyril Stapleton, if we didn't get gold records we complained of slipped discs.

Flanked by Bob Dixon and Jock Jacobsen, Jock is the non-smoker – the one with the cough.

The first flight to Australia – the pilot
did not instil confidence . . .

In 1988, on my twenty-third visit to Australia. It's the
British Government's idea – they'll keep sending me
till the Aussies take back Dame Edna Everidge.

Above – 'Oh Lord, it's hard to be humble . . .' – presented to the Queen Mother by Lord Delfont after a Royal Command Performance while Shirley Bassey looks on. *Below* – Eamonn Andrews says, 'This is your life' and guest Joe Loss says, 'My life, this is yours.'

Blossom still manages to smile after forty years.

Dame Edith once said, 'Never mind what the Press
say as long as they get your name right – remember
that Mr. Bywaters.'

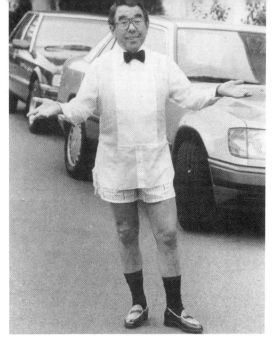

'Poor Ronnie had many personal items stolen, shoes, suits – stilts . . .'

With Tommy Cooper and Arthur Askey at a Variety Club tribute luncheon, celebrating my thirty years in show business. Tommy Cooper: 'They wanted me to stand up here today and talk about Max Bygraves – to say what a nice fellow he is, what a great entertainer he is, what a great singer he is. I said, what d'you think I am – a magician?'

'I wanna tell you a story!'

mother of the girl who worked as a chambermaid in Melbourne, whose name is Gina. A few nights ago Gina went to confession, the priest advised her to make a clean breast of it—she couldn't face you so had called her mother in Sicily to contact Mr. Sykes for forgiveness. This she was doing. I listened on the extension and, blow me, if he wasn't taken in once more.

"Meester Sickez," pleaded Jennifer, "donta letta them senda my girl to preeson pleeze."

Eric coughed, swallowed and said, "Of course not, Signora, I'll square it." I jumped in with another broken Italian accent, "You hadda betta square it Signor —else I have many Mafia friends in London who will pay a visit!"

There was a long pause, then Eric said, "You bastard!" At last he had rumbled it. When I told him everything, he said, "I have been awake almost every night worrying about that bloody bill." I don't think he thought a lot of that particular "game"; sometimes if they are too elaborate, they misfire.

Eric and I had a "gag" going on for over

thirty years—it is so childish and stupid, I am reluctant to mention it, but it makes us both smile each time one of us "scores". Back in the *Educating Archie* days, I introduced a song, "Why Does Everybody Call Me Bighead!", penned by a writer named Jack Meadows. It became a nationwide catch-phrase, with the result that a listener sent me a large cap—similar to the Andy Capp style of headgear, she told me in an accompanying letter. It had been bought at a jumble sale, their cat had kittens in it and, not knowing what to do with it, the owner had decided to send it to me, perhaps to wear during a chorus of "Bighead".

Outside the Paris Cinema in Lower Regent Street where we recorded E A, I said cheerio to Sykes, who at that time had his first car, a Ford Prefect. The back window was down and as he drove away, I threw the cap on the back seat—I thought that would be the end of it. A month later, we had lunch at Bertorelli's; he left for an appointment, I finished my coffee, paid the bill, and got my raincoat from the cloakroom. As I put my arm into the sleeve, the cap fell out—that started the gag that is still going on to this day.

On one birthday, I sent him the cap in a Harrods gift pack. Several weeks later, I was working a number in my act at the London Palladium where I used a top hat that I pick up from the piano. As I walked up stage to put on the shiny top hat, all that was there was the cloth cap. Sykes had had a word with the stage manager and got him to ring the changes. Incidentally, the cap got such a laugh that I used it throughout the run and did away with the top hat. "Maybe It's Because I'm a Londoner" had never gone better.

The cap went to and fro for many years, but the best "arrival" occurred five years ago in Tasmania. I went to the golf course where most of the theatrical profession play when in that part of the world; the pro provided clubs and buggy and also told me there were half a dozen new balls in the side pocket of the golf bag. When I got to the first tee, I unzipped the pocket he had indicated and there were half a dozen new golf balls—wrapped up in the cap.

I planted it in a Des O'Connor Show

that Eric was guest on. In front of millions, he told the history of the cap, then wore it to show how awful it looked. He "rang" it back not too long ago when there was a knock on the door at my Bournemouth home. I opened it and there in all his morning glory was the twelve-year-old paper delivery boy standing with it on. At the moment Eric wears it for a scene in a Ray Cooney farce he appears on regularly. It will turn up again in some novel way at some future date without doubt.

Jimmy Tarbuck is a good golfer, hard to beat at his handicap and fun to be with. Every game we played at Parkstone near Bournemouth, I would lose. I would then give him two new balls. At that time he was banned from driving and as I gave him the balls he handed them to his driver, who would open the boot of his car and drop the two balls in a box. This went on for quite a while. What Jimmy didn't know was that I had briefed the driver to give me the two balls back each time. When there should have been at least a dozen balls in the box, *I* won the game, Jim went to the box to pay me my two balls, and only found the two I had paid him a fortnight before. He's got a good sense of humour, saw the fun of the "game" and accepted the balls I had defaulted on. We may become friends again one day.

People in show business are fairly easy to get on with; they are like most of us, family people who don't really aim for anything else except to do their very best in the entertainment stakes and hope to make a decent living. The wages paid are the yardstick, although most of that is "pie in the sky", the income tax takes two-thirds of what you earn, so in the end we are all working for the same boss.

I got a call one morning from Bruce Forsyth. Now Bruce is a nice guy and would never think of doing anybody a bad turn. That morning, he was furious and without stopping for breath he said, "Have you seen the Sun—what do you think of that so and so—Christ, we're all in it for a living . . . there's plenty of room for everybody—why say things like that!"

I asked him who he was talking about. "Bob Monkhouse," he exploded. He then read me paragraphs of things Bob had said about most of his contemporaries who were unable to hold a candle to him (Monkhouse). I must admit, they were pretty scathing. Five minutes later, the phone rang again. It was Bob Monkhouse almost in tears. "My words have been twisted—I didn't say all those terrible things. Max, what can I do?"

Well, all you can do is to know who your interviewer is—not to be so free with your comments, remember the adage, "If you can't say something nice about someone—don't say nothing at all," because sure as hell, those Fleet Street boys *and* girls—especially the girls, will build a story up out of the smallest quote.

Newspapers cannot compete with television for news nowadays. By the time you have watched the evening news on TV, or heard the news on the hour from radio, the next day's headlines are stale. The pages have to be filled somehow and they are usually filled with gossip and interviews. If the writers can't find them, they manufacture them. We are pleased when we are acclaimed, we have to learn to "take it" when we are knocked—it is as simple as that. I have got a name for replying when I am "rubbished", but I only write when there is injustice or unfairness. Other than that they can say what they like as long as they spell the name right.

Just before last Christmas, a lady journalist called me to help her with a piece she was producing for a national newspaper. She was ringing celebrities, so she said, to find out their top ten "hates". I told her there is little in life I can find to "hate", but if she would like to hang up, call me again and ask for my top ten "dislikes", I might be able to help. She did this and I managed to come up with these . . .

1. *Foam rubber pillows*
   The very smell of them conjures up the mask the dentist put over my face as a child to take two perfectly good teeth out. I was ten at the time and could have gone through life with a couple of fillings—there were about another dozen kids in the waiting-room so I guessed he figured extractions were quickest. If I know I am going to hotels

where they are unlikely to have the feather type, I take one with me.

There must be a dozen hotels around the world who still have my feather pillows I forgot to take with me when I checked out. Blossom says she buys so many feather pillows, it would be cheaper to keep swans.

2. *Tight-fitting clothes*
There are times when I have to dress formally. I have plenty of suits but if I have to be sombre, I get hopelessly lost. I am uncomfortable in dinner jacket or tails, and will gladly give up an invitation if asked to arrive "attired suitably".

I was once refused admission to Royal Ascot because I wore an Anthony Eden instead of a top hat; a big debate followed about protocol, which went on for ten minutes. Blossom solved the problem, she said, "Come bareheaded" —why didn't we think of that?

3. *Rock music in restaurants*
The "boom bloody boom" of some youngster, screaming at the top of his

or her voice that love is going wrong for them, is not conducive to enjoying good food. I used to put up with it, now I ask the manager to turn it down. If he objects, then I leave. An Italian proprietor once asked us why we were leaving. When I told him we couldn't stand the music, he said, "I change it." We sat down again, he took off the tape of some heavy metal group to replace it with another. "How you like that—that a T Rex." "And I always thought T Rex was a margarine." Another Blossom gem.

4. *Opening milk cartons*
I have never yet succeeded in opening a milk carton without making a terrible mess. If I should ever meet the fellow who invented this in the next world I shall probably attack him with a wire coat-hanger, which is another of my dislikes.

5. *Aftershave lotion*
Until I mentioned it one Father's Day, I could have started my own pharmacy with aftershave lotion. I had thirty-

seven bottles of the stuff. The kids argued that it was difficult to come up with ideas for a man who has everything. Rubbish! I can think of a dozen things they could have sent: ICI shares, a new Rolls (my present one is nearly three years old)—*anything* except aftershave lotion, it makes me feel poofy and it makes my face smart—please kids, no more A S.

6. *TV. Quiz games*

7. *Champagne*
The songs acclaiming this brew are many; personally I prefer a well-made gin and tonic with lemon, any time. Champagne makes me liverish next day —no, I don't enjoy it any more—I did once but I don't now. Bob Dixon, my pianist, knows how to drink—a connoisseur, he sometimes goes for Black Velvet, which is Guinness and champagne; he drinks it with a feather duster in his hand—he says after six of them, it gives him something to do when he's up on the ceiling!

8. *Female Protest Singers*
What an awful whine they create as they strum their guitars and try to put the world right with their banal lyrics. I know some of them are sincere, but if I never hear another out of tune, nasal note from them, I will be happy.

9. *Mangoes*
. "Where d'ye find mangoes? Answer me boy." "Er—where woman goes?" B'boom. You also find them more and more in restaurants these days; they are used mostly as garnishing. To me, they smell of fish—nobody else can detect the smell but I have to say "No mango", like some people request "No garlic".

10. *Anything that keeps me awake*
A running tap, a loud radio in another room, a creaking floorboard, *anything*. I love my sleep, if it is interrupted or I'm too long dropping off, I am not the same person. It is the only thing in life I would be upset to lose —my ability to sleep.

I gave the lady reporter the top ten I've mentioned above; it took almost half an hour to cover. I expected to see something in print over Christmas—all I read was a line in the lady's article which simply said "Bighead Max Bygraves *hates* champagne."

16

I MUST ask the reader to forgive me if I slip out of chronological order of things and digress about some of my fellow-performers—I am, at the moment thinking of some moments shared with them that bring a smile. Danny La Rue likes to relate a story that took place in Sydney about five years ago. Danny had asked my wife, me and promoters Mr. and Mrs. Lionel Abrahams, to attend his opening night at the Regent Theatre. We sat through the show, which the audience loved, then left the auditorium to be taken backstage by his manager Jack, who looked after Danny like a mother hen. We were ushered into a separate dressing room to be lavishly plied with champagne, while Danny removed his make-up and changed from his frock. We weren't aiming to stay long because Sydney, like most other places, has a very few places to eat after 11 p.m. and we were all very hungry.

Jack, who had been with Danny for

many years, was a great diplomat and, after what must have been a quarter of an hour waiting, he told us that Danny was talking to the members of the Sydney Ballet Company. Well, we knew from the past that once Danny gets his mouth into gear, there is no stopping him. Another ten minutes went past, still no Dan.

Then Blossom, with her own particular brand of humour, said, "Good Heavens—we don't have to wait this long for the *real* Queen!"

I told Danny the line Bloss had used and next evening he put it into his show—what's more, it got one of the biggest laughs of the night.

Another incident that comes to mind was a Royal Variety Performance back in 1956. It was the year of the Suez Crisis. After rehearsing all weekend and with only two more hours to go before the Royal Family took their seats, word was received from Buckingham Palace that in view of the seriousness of the political situation, it was thought that Her Majesty should not be seen at a night out, laughing and enjoying herself. It was a great blow to us all, especially Liberace, who had given up a great deal to attend.

As you probably know, all artistes give their services free and money raised goes to help performers who have not had it so good. Liberace, accompanied by his dear old mother who did not like to fly, had crossed the United States by train from Hollywood, then in New York boarded the liner, QE2, to England—in all, about ten days' travelling.

I was sharing a dressing room with Lee, as most of us called Liberace; when I entered there he was alone, sobbing his heart out. I tried to comfort him and so did various other performers who had walked into the room. These included Winifred Atwell, Bob Monkhouse, Harry Secombe, Laurence Olivier, Dickie Henderson, Bud Flanagan, Ben Lyon, Alfred Marks, Gracie Fields and Jimmy Wheeler, a red-nosed comedian with a forceful approach.

"I think we ought to drown our sorrows," he said, as he approached the drinks cabinet, helping himself and anybody else who fancied one. With long faces, we commiserated about the situation. The only one that didn't give a hoot was Jimmy Wheeler, by now full of Scotch broth, and ready for fun. Lifting his violin case from the floor and taking out the instrument, he announced to us all, "I've been rehearsing this bleedin' act for a fortnight so somebody's gonna hear it! With that, he played the opening bars of "Mistakes", then went into his patter . . .

> "I arrived at the station carrying my props in two big cases—the ticket inspector at the gate said 'Where's your ticket?' I said, 'It's in my mouth!' So he punched me in the mouth! (Four bars of violin) I got on the train, the wife was looking out of the window—a porter said to her 'Put your head in missus— you make it look like a cattle truck!' (More violin) I said, 'That's my wife you are talking to—remember, beauty's only skin deep.' The porter said 'Blimey, don't she need skinning . . .'" (Violin solo), etc., etc.

. . . and on and on went the routine until the room, which a few minutes before was like a dentist's waiting-room, was rocking with laughter at this outrageous comedian. Liberace just looked blank—he could not believe how these crazy English performers could laugh at a moment like this.

Winifred Atwell suggested we all go to her home in north London, which we did. The last memory I have of that evening was leaving the house at 3 a.m. to the sound of "Chopsticks" being played as a duet by Winnie and Liberace.

Another Royal Variety incident, that makes me shudder, and I try to put out of my mind when the memory recurs, was the year I introduced an American girl singer to the audience by the name of Dionne Warwick. At rehearsal, I made an introduction like, "Now ladies and gentlemen, a young lady we are happy to see on these shores is our next guest, from America, Miss Dionne Warwick!"

When Miss Warwick had completed her rehearsal, she approached me to say, "When you announce me tonight, I want just Dionne Warwick—understand—nothing else, just Dionne Warwick! No embroidery—just my name!" The reason a compère embellishes an introduction is to enable the orchestra leader to put the music of the preceding act away and give the musicians time to turn over for the coming act; the few brief seconds give the stage manager time to alert the electrician so that the act walks on separated from whatever went on before.

On the night, remembering how adamant she was about her intro, I did as she requested. I shouldn't have done but I did—I walked to the centre stage, said, "Dionne Warwick" into the microphone and walked off the other side. It was chaos; it still makes me run cold. The orchestra was not ready—the lights had no time to change, the curtains didn't open, there was a stage wait that seemed like hours. Miss Warwick eventually entered to ragged applause. After that, I never listened to performers making their own arrangements. If they want that sort of introduction, they either do it themselves or get someone else to ruin their entrance.

The early part of the Sixties was a very busy time for me—although theatres were closing at an alarming rate, clubs were opening up all round the north of England, some in the south, but the grandest were in obscure towns like Batley in Yorkshire, Greasebrough, some so out of the way you needed a Himalayan Sherpa to find them.

Once, in South Shields, the most depressed town in Great Britain, I drove round the streets trying to find this place I was booked to perform at for the week. Bob Dixon and Wally Thompson, my drummer, had already left London hours before to rehearse with the band. I was due on stage at 10 p.m. and it was now nearly that. The only person I saw as I drove down the dark street was a young lady with a baby in arms, holding a heavy shopping bag. I pulled over towards her, she hurried along faster, obviously thinking I was going to proposition her. "I am looking for the Fiesta Club, can you help me?" I called loudly. She spun round shouting, "Look, if you don't stop following me, I'll call a policeman!" I felt like a dirty old kerb-crawler so decided to go round the town again, hoping to find the Fiesta Club—the whole town was empty—where on earth the girl with the baby hoped to find a policeman, I had no idea.

Suddenly, and only because I saw so many vehicles parked along the side streets, I got out of my car to investigate. I walked towards a door where a bouncer-looking type was standing; he was blowing into his hands for warmth. I asked him if he knew the whereabouts of the Fiesta Club. He said, "This is it, Max," and he opened another door for me. Then, wow! the noise of five hundred one-armed bandits filled the air—roulette tables and Las Vegas blackjack tables were in full swing. I couldn't accustom my eyes to the bright lights—I also couldn't believe I had come from the naked street into a place that rivalled Nick Sahati's at Lake Tahoe. This, in a town with an unemployment figure the highest in Britain.

They don't give much away in compliments up there either. After an hour on stage and with an enthusiastic audience demanding more, a director of the club came round to my dressing room, thrust a pint of bitter in my hand, and said, "You've took," then walked out again.

These places were small gold mines—

Jimmy Corrigan, who owned the Batley Variety Club, built the place in nine weeks, it seated 1500 people. His first booking was Louis Armstrong, his second was the Hallé Orchestra. He booked every top act in the land. Patrons travelled from as far away as Edinburgh, two hundred miles or more, for an evening out. I saw Jimmy being interviewed on television not too long ago, unable to explain why the bubble burst. I can't think why either, looking back there is no earthly reason why the club shouldn't have remained a way of life for the British working man for ever. The drink was reasonably priced, the food was adequate, the entertainment was especially good and Jimmy was a fine business man.

With the demise of Batley, most of the other clubs folded. We had to find other fields to plough. I took a booking in South Africa that Jock Jacobsen had fixed. When I told Eve Boswell, a South African by birth, and former singer with the Geraldo orchestra, she said, "Go, Max—please— you'll love it." The apartheid question was very subdued at that time, the only inkling we had that South Africa was out of bounds was that the Musicians Union frowned on members going there. My drummer at the time was Martin Aston; he had accompanied me on engagements all over the world but would not come to South Africa. "Max—I've just got married —if the union finds out I've been there, I will be blacklisted and I can't afford it!" He had quite a valid argument, even though later on, he got a job on one of the ships, got off at Cape Town—loved the place—sent for his wife and settled down there—still lives there—I get a Christmas card from him every year, he would not return for love or money. *I was in Johannesburg last week—they provided me with two pianos—one with black notes one with white. Rest assured your government will remain the same, even the pigeons in the square keep saying "Verwoerd! Verwoerd! Verwoerd!"*

Verwoerd was the Prime Minister at the time. He was assassinated in 1966; that was the extent of political friction at that period, mostly to the visitor everything was peaceful and we did our work under the most wonderful conditions. The butt of the South African jokes there was a mythical figure known as Van de Merwe, pronounced Van de Merva—all you needed to do to make South Africans fall about with laughter was to swap every Irish joke around to V de Ms, here's an example:

Van de Merva went to London, stayed at the Dorchester Hotel. He walked into the bar and saw this very attractive lady sitting there; he asked the barman to give her a drink with V de M's compliments.
The barman said, "You are wasting your time, she is a Lesbian."
V de M. insisted, the barman gave her a champagne cocktail with the South African's compliments—now Van de Merwe makes his way towards her with a big smile, saying ". . . and what part of Lesbia do you come from?"
(Cymbal crash Wally)

I find it hard to be uncomplimentary towards South Africa, mostly because each time I have been there, apart from a couple of incidents, we have had a grand time. Friends like Mona and Mossie Berman have given us the freedom of their homes. I know there is an underlying current about the injustice to the blacks and coloureds, it's just that I don't feel I am able to do a damned thing about it. The country belongs to the South Africans. We allowed them to govern it the way they think fit, they think they are doing it right and while the world is governed by the financial giants who need and trade in gold, it will be the same. We, the people, are manipulated by these predators, the diamonds and that yellow metal are mined at such low wages, but to me it seems the governments of the world don't want it changed.

It came home to me when Idi Amin was in power in Uganda—a gag I was working about this butcher, was to the effect that he had to be hospitalised. *"The doctor that gave him an enema had to roll him in flour to find out where his bum was."*

I was told politely but firmly to leave it out . . . then Idi Amin was overthrown, all his crimes were listed when he fled to Libya, I thought it would be all right to put it back in on a future visit, but no— they were afraid of upsetting Gaddafi, can you imagine? But before I stopped going there, I had some entertaining visits. One incident occurred on the golf course when I partnered Bobby Locke, five times Open golf champion, just outside Johannesburg. Bobby was a lovely man, our opponents were also nice guys—British golfers Brian Barnes and Hedley Muscroft. We were playing for £10 a hole and we were one up at the sixteenth. As I approached my tee shot, which had made the centre of the fairway, Bobby said, "Steady master (he called everybody master), take your five wood and hit it straight at the green." I told him I didn't have a five wood in my bag and he said I could borrow his. To my amazement, the ball finished three inches from the pin. The money was ours.

In the club house, Bobby was as pleased as Punch at my great shot (you get few of those in a lifetime at my handicap). "Why haven't you got a five wood, master, you used it so wonderfully," enthused Bobby.

I told him that when I returned to the UK I would buy one.

"Don't do that, master—I will write to

Lillywhite's in Piccadilly Circus—when you are next in London, pop in and there will be a five wood waiting for you." Bobby was notoriously forgetful, owing to a nasty accident when his car stalled on a railway crossing previously, so I didn't give it a lot of thought.

I returned to London and several weeks later I happened to be passing Lillywhite's. I thought I had better inquire if Bobby had contacted them—perhaps he had remembered. The salesman told me indeed they had heard from the great man and that it was there ready to be wrapped. I watched him put the brown paper and Sellotape round, then give it to me with, "That will be eight pounds ten shillings, please Mr. Bygraves."

That is not the end of the story. That day I came up to London by train from Leatherhead. I had to return in the rush hour, and as I pushed my way into the crowded carriage at Waterloo, with the wrapped golf club held tight, a porter shouted, "Mind the doors." He then slammed the carriage door right on to the end of the protruding club—result, the head of the club dangling from the twine.

I still haven't got a five wood in my golf set, but I have beautiful memories of Bobby, who sadly passed away in March 1987.

The caddies we used in South Africa were young chaps, usually in their early teens. On one particular course, belonging to the East Rand Gold Mine Company, I was having a bad day with my drives, slicing or hooking into the rough. Each time my native caddy went in to search for the ball, he would sing loudly and clap in rhythm. I remarked to George Farmer, the pro I was playing with, how happy they were, singing and clapping as they did their job. "Happy nothing," said George, ". . . they do that to drive the snakes ahead of them." Funny how a remark like that can make you keep your tee shot straight.

In Cape Town, I was in the locker-room showering, when my partner introduced me to a prominent politician. This gentleman was keen to know what the South African image was around the world. I told him that it might get greater acceptance if performers like myself were allowed to play to black audiences. He was amazed that we should think it was taboo. "There is nothing stopping you from doing that if you wish," he said.

I mentioned this to Mr. Quibell, the promoter of most concerts in South Africa. He too was amazed that I would want to —"I can arrange it—I own a theatre in the coloured section called the Luxurama."

The following week, I became one of the first white performers to appear in front of a coloured audience in South Africa. The media got wind of it, the press corps arrived to get pictures, rolls and rolls of film were taken of what to them was a historic moment—and not one picture made the papers—not there, or back in the United Kingdom. I don't know what it is like now, it is four years since I was last there, but I find most individuals from that country are usually rather nice people. It is their argument that, with eighteen million blacks and just over three million whites, they wouldn't have a chance of survival if the balance of power shifted.

I go to see movies like *Cry Freedom*, made by sincere filmmaker Dickie Attenborough—I watch well-meaning television

256

documentaries that tell me of South Africa's faults—what I am waiting for is somebody to come up with a solution of how to create a society in that country without the tragedy the present one is experiencing, then perhaps I might be able to contribute in some way.

17

URING the Sixties, I was asked to
go to Israel by the Variety Club
of Great Britain. The idea was to
present a Sunshine Coach to some needy
children in Jerusalem; it was just after the
Six Day War. The roads were strewn with
knocked-out tanks that had been pulled to
the edge of the main thoroughfares and left
to rust.

The party I was with was entertained by
dignitaries who included Moshe Dyan and
General Herzog. I was there to entertain
in cabaret after a dinner to be given in our
(the Variety Club's) honour at the lavish
Tel Aviv Hilton ballroom. It was at this
bash I think I saw the most stunning, the
most beautiful and most voluptuous creature I have ever seen—and I have met
many beautiful women—her name was
Bianca, she was from Nicaragua and later
married Mick Jagger of the Rolling Stones.
On this particular night, she wore a gold
balaclava-type helmet that joined a gold

dress of the same material; she walked as the model she was and the gasp from the all Jewish audience as she made her way to the top table could be heard all over Tel Aviv. *"I wanted to go to the Wailing Wall"—I said to the taxi-driver—"Take me to the place where the Jews cry." He took me to the income tax office!—I travelled with El Al Airlines—they don't have young attractive stewardesses—they have little old ladies with bowls of locshen soup walking up and down the aisle saying, "Eat it up, it's good for you!"*

The most popular "story" I told was of the new soldier in the Israeli Army who asked for seven days' leave; they told him he wouldn't get that until he did something really heroic. "Like what?" he asked. "Like capturing an enemy tank," he was told.

Next day, he drove into camp with an enemy tank. "Do I get my seven days' leave?" he asked. "Of course—but how did you do it?" The young soldier told them he went down to the frontier—on the other side was an Arab in an enemy tank—I called out to him, "How would you like seven days' leave?" . . . he said he would *love* seven days' leave, so I shouted, "Swap tanks!"

The following day, we were told we would be taken to the desert home of Ben-Gurion, a much-loved statesman and one of the architects of Israel. After driving for quite a long time across brown desert sand, we came to this small residence that had trees and greenery around it, an experiment by Mr. Ben-Gurion to prove that things can grow in the desert.

This white-haired, frail man with alert eyes and sharp humour, welcomed us members of the Variety Club who were mostly of the Jewish faith. I think that Michael Caine and I were the only two "goys" (Christians) there.

Mr. Ben-Gurion invited questions: somebody asked what he would like to see for Israel before he was called by his Maker. His reply has stayed with me ever more; it made such a lot of sense. He told us that during the Second World War, he served with the British government as adviser on Middle East affairs. It was the practice to go to the Houses of Parliament on Sunday mornings up till midday. When he was through, he took a stroll up

Victoria Street to Hyde Park, to listen to the orators at Speakers' Corner. Now, there was a heavy war going on, England was almost on its knees, yet there were men on soapboxes telling the crowd that Adolf Hitler was a *good* man—the moment we stopped warring with him and joined his campaign, the better it would be for Britain.

Ben-Gurion wasn't concerned with the orators' ideals; what impressed him more was the fact that a man could, with a war going on, stand there, praise the enemy and yet not be led off to the Tower of London to be shot as a traitor. Added Mr. Ben-Gurion: "There is not one country I can think of where a man could do that and get away with it—that is democracy —when that kind of democracy comes to Israel, we will have the country I envisage."

Jock Jacobsen, my manager, was with me on this trip. One afternoon, I sat on Mount Scopus looking down on Jerusalem. I was addressing some Christmas cards to friends around the world. Jock asked me why I was sending them from there and not from home in England. I explained to him that Bethlehem was where the birth of Jesus Christ took place and that to receive a card from there would be like getting one from "headquarters". He thought this a great idea. He rushed into the hotel and purchased a dozen cards; at the same time we were called for a guided tour of the walled city.

As our guide fascinated us with tales that we had read only in our Bibles, it did not seem possible we were now standing on the actual soil trodden by Jesus and his disciples. Jock was busily addressing his cards to send to clients and relatives. When he had finished, he saw a red pillarbox with GR and a crown embossed on the front. He posted his cards in the box. A young Arab youth asked him what he had done with the cards; Jock told him he had posted them. "That box hasn't been emptied since the British were here," said the youth.

Jock, whose handwriting was never all that legible, said, "They'll probably open the post box up in two thousand years, find the cards and swear they are the Dead

Sea Scrolls." The cards have never arrived.

On returning to London, Jock asked me if I would like to work at the Chequers Nightclub in Sydney, Australia. This was owned by a Chinese gentleman named Denis Wong, a likeable dapper chap with "stories" that have become legend, like the time he was taken by an agent to see the Beatles at the Horden Pavilion. At that time they were nothing like the name they were to become. Denis sat there impassive as the kids around him screamed and cried to the foursome on stage. The agent, who was hoping that Denis would book their next tour, asked, "What do you think?" Denis replied "I like them—I take two."

I signed for four weeks to appear at Denis's place. It was for two shows nightly. The first show was a doddle, it began at 7.30 p.m. with a lovely family audience. The second show was around midnight, where the racing fraternity and the dregs of Sydney, many spending money they had plundered, were killing time before an all-night session of poker. I drew this particular crowd to Chequers, which pleased Denis tremendously. He told me the difference in the "take" at the end of the week compared to say, a singing act group like the Three Degrees, was many thousands of pounds, the reason being that followers of that type of act drank Coca Cola, whereas my crowd were asking for French champagne at sixty dollars a bottle. Easy come—easy go!

Two weeks into the engagement, I was called from London to say that my father was very ill and was not expected to last the week. I told Denis, who was most sympathetic and arranged for a "dep". I caught the next plane to London. After the long flight, I motored out to Abbey Wood where my family were gathered round him, waiting for the end. A faint smile of recognition came into his eyes as I held his hand. He was never a big man, but the body he had always been so proud of had shrunk to a five-stone bag of bones. The pressure on my hand told me he was happy to see me. I made it by about three hours, then he passed on.

Apart from Grandfather, who died during the Blitz, there had never been a death in the family, so it was left to me to make most of the arrangements. My mother was in a quandary but, luckily, all my sisters apart from Lily lived near by so she had plenty of people to comfort her. After the funeral, I caught the next plane to Sydney to honour the contract with Denis Wong at Chequers. From freezing to 97°F.

To tackle the thirty-six hour journey, as it was then, twice in under a week was madness. Very few people's metabolism can handle it, to try it there and back and work to an audience twice nightly is stupid, but it had to be done. I actually sat in the dressing room one evening and fell asleep just before the second show. I was awakened by banging on the door where Bob Dixon, wide-eyed, was saying, "Listen, the crowd are slow handclapping —I've already played your entrance music —get dressed quickly." I did—and worked like a zombie for the hour I was required to perform. Bob said I have never worked better, but I assured him it was "painting by numbers".

I finished at Chequers, said goodbye to my daughter Christine and her two babies, Michael and Louise. She had told me previously she had found a young man, an artist, she was very fond of named Barry. If he got round to popping the question, not to be surprised if wedding bells started chiming. She was still in her mid-twenties so we were expecting something of the sort one day.

I played a few dates around England, plus a couple of "Five Past Eight Shows" in Glasgow. After this, I was asked to appear on the Jackie Gleason Show from Miami. I flew there and went over well—so much so, that as I returned home and touched down at Heathrow, Jock was waiting with a telegram in his hand. It was from the Gleason office saying that owing to the "smash" appearance the week before, would I return for the following Friday night show. He had the tickets at the ready if I felt like turning round again. I did—about twelve hours later, I was back in the Gleason office rehearsing for Friday night's show—it was now Wednesday.

Jackie Gleason was a big, overweight man, who had a permanent mischievous glint in his eye. He could swear with words I had never heard before, he began drinking about 10 a.m. and went through until 5 p.m. I once played golf with him in Miami—we had a golf cart with our clubs on the back. In front of him he had not one but two quarts of martinis in cardboard pint pots *and* when we got to the ninth, a boy was waiting to replenish *both* cartons. I liked Jackie a lot, there was something going on inside him that told one he was not a secure man. He needed a friend who was a listener because he talked most of the time, as long as it was show business he was happy—he was a lousy golfer but he liked the cart and one listener. Sometimes he'd be too lazy to get off the golf cart, he'd just say, "You hit the ball for me!" If you struck it well, he'd say, "Hey—didn't I hit a good one!" There was no way he could reach a ripe old age—not after he had abused his body the way he did—but he was quite philosophical about it. The glint in his eye would become brighter as he'd say, "We've all got to go."

On the strength of my two previous appearances, it was offered to me to take over the show as a summer replacement; this was for eight weeks while Jackie took a vacation. It was probably the biggest accolade a British artiste could have bestowed on him. With Bob Dixon, and a small allowance from the Bank of England because sterling still could not be taken out in bulk, we left for Miami to conquer America; this was the summer of 1967. We were given four comedy writers—the line of dancing girls remained, my first guest was to be Kim Novak. Rehearsals went smoothly and we were full of confidence for the first show, some of the dialogue with Kim Novak went like this . . .

Max: Were you ever in England, Kim?
Kim: Yes, I once stayed in Birming*ham*.
Max: No Kim, it isn't pronounced *"ham"*, it is hummmmm—Birminghummmmm.
Kim: I stayed at a nice hotel and had a fabulous breakfast.
Max: What did you have?
Kim: Hummmm and eggs.
Max: I would dearly love to be in a picture with you.
Kim: That could be arranged.
Max: Really—how?
Kim: Like this. (Man appears with

Polaroid camera, snaps Max and Kim together, gives the picture to Max, who looks at it)
Max: Let's go into the darkroom and see what develops.
(They exit)
Cue for music, "If I Had a Talking Picture"

It was pretty tepid stuff but I was assured that by the time "McKenzie" had been added, it would be belly-laughs. I found out that McKenzie was the name of a technician who had invented a tape filled with audience laughter—to boost laughs, the tape loop was allowed to run and amplified at the press of a button. This was married to the video then, *voilà!* a riotous comedy show without too much effort. As a matter of fact, a puppeteer named Shari Lewis told me that she arrived late at the studio a few weeks before because of an air strike. She did her act with her puppet, Lamb Chop, in an empty studio, McKenzie added his laugh track and Shari's parents phoned her to say they had watched the TV show and never seen her better *and* "didn't the audience love it". Very few shows from America work without a track now but Jackie Gleason's outfit was among the first to use one.

We rehearsed until a few hours before going on air, then a bombshell—musicians all over the United States decided to strike for more money, the show was cancelled along with almost every other musical show on television, and we sat twiddling our thumbs until the following Friday—even then, it wasn't settled.

The contract became null and void because of industrial dispute. I was paid the first two shows but after that, nothing. With the hotel bill, air fares and Inland Revenue taking their cut, we had to think of something. I was staying at the Deauville Hotel on Miami Beach; this hotel was used by BOAC crews. A pilot advised me to cross over to Nassau in the Bahamas, which was only twenty minutes or so by air from Miami. I could sit the strike out there because Nassau was in the sterling area at that period, so I would be able to use as much British currency as I wished until I resumed work on the Gleason Show. I didn't know that the strike was to last for another eleven weeks, in fact it was thirteen in all before it was settled. I left an address in Nassau where I could be contacted, and from where I could be back in Miami in an hour or so when the musicians' dispute was settled. It was a big loss to me because I was to be paid $8,000 per show over eight weeks; instead of that I was getting nothing, waiting for the phone call that didn't come. I often wonder if I had bothered to follow it through, whether I would have become a name in the US—now I don't suppose I'll ever know.

Jackie died last year but I'm told that he went quite cheerfully; his catchphrase, "How Sweet It Is" sums up the man.

Another stalwart of show business whom I got to know intimately around that time was Jack Benny. Jack was totally different to Gleason, a quiet man who, like most of us, wanted to do a competent job. I first got to know him in 1952 when he invited me to his apartment in New York. At this time he was very hot on radio and with support from Rochester, Dennis Day and Mary Livingstone (Jack's wife), he was making the transition from radio to TV and was worried about it.

I had used a penguin on a television show in Britain and Jack loved the lines I was using about this show-stealer, lines like, "Clever birds these penguins—look at the books they write," or, "Careful, if you buy one of these—you can't always get the batteries," or, ". . . looks like Mickey Rooney at one of his weddings".

When I told Jack about the laughter I had raised with the camera dwelling on the bird which I called Percy, Jack asked me if he could use the idea. I told him to go ahead, it was an enormous success—for this he presented me with a gold money clip engraved "From Jack to Max" with a further engraving on the other side of Jack in one of his many hand-clasped poses. I use it almost every day so hardly twenty-four hours go by when I don't think of him.

I appeared twice on his television programme from Hollywood and spent quite a lot of time at his house. One evening, Mary, his wife, took the dog out for a walk round the block. When she returned, Jack and I were sitting in the lounge, each smoking a cigar. Mary had just bumped into James Stewart, who was also walking his dog. It seemed that so many impressionists were impersonating Stewart's drawl, he had become a caricature of himself, and when Mary asked after his health Jimmy went into "Er—well—er—Mary—I er—er . . ." She said to him, "Look Jimmy, I just want to know how you are, I don't want an impression." Then she hurried past.

Jack was flabbergasted. "Oh Mary—you didn't . . ." As he put his hand to his face the way his television audience knew him best, Mary went on ". . . and there's no need for you to do an impression of Jack Benny either!" The dog began to to bark loudly, she waved a finger at it and said, "And you can cut out your impression of Ethel Merman!"

Mary was a dominant figure who was ever-protective of Jack. One day she called him from New York to tell him that she had been attacked and robbed in her hotel on 5th Avenue. It was most frightening; as she and her maid entered the suite, two men jumped them, told them they would not get hurt if they handed over their money and jewellery. Mary was wearing a $25,000 diamond ring, which was taken by the bandits with some smaller items kept in the bedroom. Afterwards, they were tied to chairs back to back and told not to make a sound, and the robbers left.

When they had freed themselves, Mary gave the manager of the hotel a piece of her mind. She then phoned Jack in Los Angeles to tell him of the fright she had endured. The New York papers made it their cover story. The very next day, she phoned Jack again, and he related what she had said almost word for word. "Jack, I went through a traumatic experience yesterday—now, they say that if you are learning to ride a horse and get thrown, the best thing to do is mount again quickly, try to forget the experience—so Jack, I am going to put yesterday's robbery out of my mind. This morning I went round to Tiffany's and bought a new diamond ring—it cost $40,000 but I feel confident again." Jack got a great deal of pleasure telling that "story" through the years, and it always came up fresh.

On other occasions, Jack would take me

to Hillcrest Golf Club, an exclusive course quite near Beverly Hills. There is a large table overlooking the eighteenth green that is reserved for the showbiz fraternity. Almost any day you could find stars like Danny Thomas, George Burns, Groucho Marx, Bob Hope and more, topping each other's jokes. It was here I was to meet and become friends with a pal of Jack's, George Burns. Every Wednesday for the past twenty years, I have looked at "Milestones" in my *Time* magazine expecting to read of his passing, but up till now he just keeps celebrating birthdays; his last one was his ninety-second. When I asked George to fly from LA to London to be a guest on my TV programme *LingalongaMax*, I expected him to beg off because of age—not a bit of it. With his manager, Irving Fein, he made the trip with ease. When I met him at Heathrow, he looked fit enough to take on Muhammed Ali, and he was nearly eighty then!

For ten days, he told "stories" without repeating himself once. He kept me and the production staff enthralled with tales that he made so colourful and real; let's see if I can remember some of those vaudeville days he spoke of—imagine it's George telling it . . .

(George talking) The greatest act I ever worked with was George M. Cohan—we did five shows a day then—the audience would be round the block queueing for the next performance as the one before was starting—he was the greatest attraction in America.
(Stop for a few puffs at cigar)
On the bill, were two male hoofers (dancers). They had only just started in the business and were wide-eyed at being on the same bill as the legendary Cohan.
(Look at the cigar ash, taps into ashtray)
During the change-over from one audience to the next, we used the bar for a drink or coffee, or whatever, the two dancers, still unable to believe their good fortune at being chosen for a George M. Cohan Show, approached the great man to say, "Mr. Cohan, this is the thrill of a lifetime for us, to be working with you—it would give us great pleasure if we could buy you a drink." Cohan said to them in a choked voice,

"Thanks fellas, but I'd rather drink alone—I have just received this telegram to tell me I have lost my mother." One of the dancers in genuine sympathy said, "We know how you feel, Mr. Cohan—two weeks ago we lost our suitcase."

George Burns would smile at the thought, then go on to explain that to a touring performer, his suitcase was his home, his toilet, his comfort in digs—without your suitcase you had nothing, no props, no belongings—nothing. He told me how, as a small boy, he would go into one of those new quick service automats where you put in ten cents, a flap opened, and you took your hot soup. With a clever bit of thinking and a paper clip, he would take the soup for his ten cents, then wedge the paper clip in such a way that he could go back, lift the flap . . . "and," I chimed in, ". . .have two lots of soup". George told me that he not only had two bowls of soup —he was selling soup round the restaurant for five cents a dish.

I said, "That was stealing." He said, "If you didn't steal—you didn't eat—if you didn't eat, you starved to death . . ." (Tap of cigar in ash tray) ". . . think what Gracie would have missed.

"I take *Variety* every week, I open the page at Obituaries; if I'm not mentioned, I get up.

"I had a dressing room right next to the dancing girls—somebody had drilled a hole to spy through. I'm nearly eighty—things like that don't worry me—if they want to look, let 'em look."

When Jack Benny and George Burns were together, it was like having a front seat at a vaudeville show.

One evening, the two of them had dinner at Chasens in Beverly Hills, a restaurant frequented by many of the big Hollywood stars. George tapped my knee under the table to signal to me he was about to play a joke on Jack. He lit a fresh cigar, then said, "Jack, we have been coming to this restaurant for twenty years —many people come in just to stare at us —at other times we have brought large parties with us—yet not once has the owner ever said, 'Have this dinner on me —I'll pay the bill'." Jack agreed that Dave Chasen had never picked up the tab.

George continued: "Tonight when he

brings the bill, whoever he gives it to, let the other one of us say, 'I'll pay that'. If he then gives it to the other one of us, say 'If *he* pays that bill *I* will never use this restaurant again.' If he presents the other one with it, 'And if *he* pays it I will never come here again.' He will be so embarrassed he will have to tear the goddam bill up."

After coffee, Dave Chasen came to the table, then laid the bill in front of George Burns. Jack immediately said, "If you let him pay that bill I will never come into this restaurant again." Chasen picked up the check and laid it in front of Jack, whereupon George just went on puffing his cigar, looking at the ceiling. Jack fell about laughing as he realised that he had been set up by Burns—George had phoned earlier and arranged it. They had dozens more of these elaborate jokes, they were the greatest of pals.

Jack was to star in *The Sunshine Boys*, but he died before it was ready for shooting. Irving Fein secured the part for Burns and it started a new movie career for George who is still, up to the time of writing, very much in demand. One of

George's lines that stays with me is when he was talking about the death of Eddie Cantor: somebody asked if he left much: George replied, "Everything."

18

PROBABLY the most rewarding thing about becoming known in the entertainment industry is the way one contact leads to another; when I wrote "You Need Hands", I was given the Ivor Novello Award for the effort. At the dinner for the presentation of the awards, I met Lou Levy, a vey successful music publisher from USA—at that time married to Maxine of the Andrews Sisters fame.

Lou made an attractive offer for the American rights to the song, got an immediate recording by Eydie Gormé and, in less than two months, had a hit. We became, and still are, good friends. Even though the music scene is worlds away from what it was in the Fifties, I still believe that Lou is capable of making hit material, providing he is given the goods to work with. His bright blue eyes and ready smile make one want to claim him as a friend. During dinner one night at the 21 Club I mentioned I was on my way to

Hawaii. "When you are there . . ." said Lou ". . . contact a friend of mine—his name is Aku—he's a great guy—you'll love him." Over the next twenty years, after meeting Aku, I did indeed "love" him, we became firm friends, so much so, I would arrange my travel to go to Honolulu as often as I could; at one time I lived among the Hawaiians for a long period. Aku and I met almost every day. Later, when he came to England for the first time, we lived "in each other's pockets". Aku was not his real name; this was Hal Lewis. During the war, he served with the US Forces in the Pacific —demobilised after hostilities, he was put down in Honolulu. He had compèred shows for the troops, read bulletins over the Tannoy, so that when he picked up the *Honolulu Advertiser* and saw an ad for a news reader he applied and got the job on what he called "the coconut wireless". He was an instant success and became the pioneer of the "phone-in".

During one of these phone-ins, an irate Hawaiian called Hal "Aku!", which freely translated means "Fish Head"! Hal kept the name and was known to the natives simply as Aku. A worldly man with a great knowledge of politics and show business, having at one time played violin with the Kay Kyser Band, he settled down in Hawaii and loved the islands dearly. Every morning from six o'clock until ten, Aku kept the airwaves from station KGMB sizzling with entertainment. At one time he was rated as America's highest-paid disc-jockey. Calls would come in from housewives asking him to find their stray dog or cat—how to feed parrots, whether he thought Spiro Agnew was a crook, are there too many Japanese taking over Honolulu, and so on.

With his fine resonant voice Aku would come up with an opinion that usually summed up the question. After listening to him one morning fielding the most banal calls, I decided to give him a buzz. Putting on a simple American accent, I said, "Aku, I need your help—my wife went shopping, and before she left she asked me to clean the goldfish bowl, I had to put Harry somewhere—Harry is the name of our goldfish—not having any other place to put him, I decided to put him into the lavatory bowl, clean *his* bowl, then return Harry to it nice and bright."

Aku listened patiently, then asked why I needed his help. I continued—he never suspected it was me—"I was about to take Harry from the toilet, when the phone rang—I had a long conversation with the caller—in the meantime, my wife had returned from shopping, let herself in, gone straight to the bathroom, used the toilet then flushed it, flushing Harry away." There was a long pause from Aku, who knew most of the cranks that called, but couldn't place this one. "I don't see how I can help," he ventured.

Using the same voice, I carried on. "Well, Harry is probably flushed out to sea and is there at the moment—I was wondering if the man in the helicopter that reports the traffic and weather each morning, could keep an eye out for Harry . . ."

"You've got to be kidding," said Aku. If you heard some of the inquiries he had to contend with, this was quite a reasonable request.

The two of us kept it up for a few more minutes until I boobed with the word "chance", he heard me slip and use the English pronunciation "charnce". Then he knew, but we kept the goldfish saga going for several weeks.

On the first trip to Honolulu, I arrived with quite an entourage. There was Bloss, my three children, also two young grand-children and nanny Kathy. We checked into the Hilton Hawaiian Village, which was delightful, but after being presented with the first week's bill I knew I was going to have a problem making ends meet, especially as I had promised them a four-week vacation. I had my Australian earnings but I knew that would soon go— sterling was still restricted from the UK. Something had to be done, the air fares alone had left me skint. Reading the classi-fieds in the *Advertiser*, I spotted an ad for "a five-bedroom house situated on the edge of a lagoon with all amenities $200 per week". A vast difference from the $1,000 weekly it was costing at the Hawaiian Village Hotel. With Bloss we taxied out to a spot called Kaneohe, some fifteen miles from Waikiki Beach. The lady renting the place had just been granted a divorce and was impatient to get back to mainland US with her two young children. When I promised to keep the house in good hands she replied, "Do what you want with it—burn it, if you like!" She was a very unhappy female.

The next day, our crowd moved in. It was a spacious house with large pool, barbecue, bar, stereo on the patio, plenty of bedrooms, oh yes, and for the $200 rental, she included a maid and the station wagon.

One day, with nothing to do, I noticed what a sorry state the house was getting into through not being looked after. Paint was peeling, doors were off hinges, windows were not closing. It was because the woman who rented it to us probably had not had a man about the house to do these odd jobs. I decided to help. I went to the shops and bought a few tools, hammer, screwdrivers, spanners and screws. I made a lot of the faults good again, then set to work on a rowing-boat that we wanted to use but couldn't because one of the rowlocks was missing. A rowlock is what holds the oars, it allows you to exert pressure on the oar. I figured that if I inserted two six-inch screws about four inches apart, then bound the top of them with wire, it would work as a rowlock; we would then be able to row on the lagoon.

I did this and made a reasonable job of it—I put the boat into the lagoon and began to row. When I was a couple of hundred yards out, the pressure was too much and the screws gave way. As I turned to pull in the oar on the side that had the good rowlock, the other oar slid into the water. I was in a swim suit, so I decided to jump in and retrieve it. It had floated a good few yards from the rowing-boat. The first thing I noticed as I got in the water was a very strong undercurrent. I am a fairly good swimmer and struck out for the boat, pushing the oar in front of me. I made the boat, panting like an old bull, and threw the oar up into the boat.

If I can give advice at this stage, be guided by me and never try to get back into a rowing-boat without somebody to help you. You will wear yourself out and find that it is practically impossible. There was no way I could get back in that rowing-boat without up-ending it.

I yelled to my kids who were oblivious of me out there in the lagoon; they were playing records on a radiogram by the pool and could hear nothing. Meanwhile, I was getting weaker. I decided to swim, pushing the boat in front of me, but it was heavy going in the current, also I was drifting farther and farther away from the house.

I yelled louder and louder, but nobody could hear me, then I noticed I was drifting towards another large house—if I could steer towards that, it was about my last hope before I went out to sea. By some strength I mustered, I managed to make the bottom of the garden of the house.

Nobody could hear my cry for help. I pulled myself up and as I did, my chest scraped on the coral. I got out and saw that I was bleeding from my neck to my knees. As I lay there thankful to be where I was, out of the mess I had been in, down the garden lunged a large Alsatian dog, all ready to turn me into a mid-morning meal.

"Oh Christ!" I thought, "please don't make me go back in that water." Luckily, there was a chain-link fence that kept him away, although he kept charging the fence. All I had to sit on was about eighteen inches of soil so his jowls were only a few inches from my face each time he charged.

I was still, for some reason that I have never figured out to this day, holding the rowing-boat by the rope.

I had to make a decision, finish up as Pal Meat or get back into the boat. I pulled the boat as near as I could, then jumped in, just as the hound broke the fence. I hung on to the oar, ready to knock him senseless if he decided to jump too. It took me ages to manipulate the boat with one oar back to the house—eventually, I did it. I stepped off on to the little jetty, covered in blood which was flowing freely from my chest. I decided to get into the pool and wash it clean. As I was doing this, Blossom came out, saw me in the pool, and said, "Come along, Max—lunch is ready. I've been calling you for an hour!" I thought, "Yes, and I've been bloody well calling you for two!"

When I got out of the pool, she saw the blood and almost fainted. I got injected against the possibility of coral poisoning a little later and I *did* faint—I always do when I see a syringe going into my arm.

Last year, I decided to surprise Aku and arrived unannounced. I booked into the

Royal Hawaiian Hotel, with my week planned. Blossom would go shopping at the Ala Moana, her favourite pastime (she buys so many things for the grandchildren, they must think she is married to a pop star). I could go to the golf course with Aku, then we'd go out in the evening to those wonderful restaurants like the Third Floor or my friend's Italian restaurant.

On the way in from the airport, I chatted to the Hawaiian taxi driver. "How's Aku?" I asked. "Aku? He dead," he replied. My friend from station KGMB had passed on two months before and I did not know. It wasn't the same Hawaii and we cut our holiday short by five days. I really do miss the man. So many tracks did he play from my albums, which he genuinely liked, a listener once phoned in to ask if Station KGMB stood for Keep Getting Max Bygraves.

19

SHORTLY after returning from the US, I played a season at the Winter Gardens Theatre in Bournemouth—how I loved that town, still do. I rented a place for the ten-week duration of the show and enjoyed the place even more each day. I had previously bought a house at Torquay; that was also a lovely town, with a gorgeous view of Thatcher Rock. The fault with Torquay was there were no motorways at that time. It took five hours to reach—so when we saw the house on the cliff edge at Bournemouth we bought it, then sold the one in Torquay. It originally had ten bedrooms, but by the time Blossom had knocked a few walls down, she turned it into six bedrooms en suite. We had a swimming pool put in—a billiard room—a projection room and a gymnasium.

It was the meeting-place for the Bygraves clan. My sister Lily lived around the corner with her husband Arthur and he helped to build it into a beautiful "first-class residence", which it wasn't when we moved in.

In later years, I was able to invite other artistes playing the theatres in the town to use the pool—play snooker—or just laze in the lovely garden.

The episode that many people remember was when I had to be rescued when hanging down the cliff at Bournemouth; it happened like most stupid accidents happen. I was flying a kite at the bottom of the garden for Michael, my first grandson. The wind dropped, the kite fell to earth, missed the garden and caught a branch about twelve feet down the cliff-face. Michael, who was about nine, was quite upset about the loss. To pacify him, I said I would go down the cliff to get it. I took a plastic clothes-line down from the posts, secured it to a tree, then put it round me, under my legs commando-style. I tested it with my weight and descended the cliff, which is quite sheer with over a one-hundred-foot drop. I got the kite, secured it to the clothes-line and tried to get back; this wasn't as easy. I weigh just over thirteen stone (around 190lb), it was summer, my hands were moist and as I tried to climb up the line, they just slid back. My toes were pressed hard into the soft cliff-face as I tried to figure out how to manage the ascent.

Michael, by now, had got fed up waiting for the return of his 29p kite and went back into the house to eat. It wasn't until a good ten minutes later somebody at the dinner table, asked, "Where's Gramps?" Between mouthfuls of food, Michael told them I was hanging down the cliff-face—a great practical joker and kidder, nobody took any notice of him. Meanwhile, the line was cutting into my hands, the rope under my fork was turning me into a soprano and I was wondering why I had never got round to making a will.

Even Michael got worried about me not sitting down at the table and he managed to convince the other diners I *was* hanging from a tree at the bottom of the garden. They came to look. Blossom's first words were "What are you playing at?" I was the nearest I have ever been to leaving this world and she's asking me what I was *playing* at.

I tried not to panic, told her quietly that I couldn't get up the cliff and that I needed help. She flew into action and called the fire station which, luckily, is at the end of our road. It seemed like an eternity that I hung there trying to figure out whether I should fall on my back, which I was certain to break, or swing round and crash down to the promenade face first.

The fire brigade arrived, looked down at me hanging there, then came on with all the gags. One started singing, "You Need Hands . . ." Another one said, "Go on Max—tell us a story." I thought, "Christ, I can only manage a few more minutes and these life-savers are doing 'funnies'."

They lowered a thick hawser-type rope, which I took, and was back on terra firma in a few seconds. The firemen stayed for a drink and almost immediately, the phone began to ring. First the local Bournemouth *Echo*, then the Press Association asking to confirm a report that Max Bygraves had tried committing suicide from the top of the cliff. Everything turned out well but I was unable to hold a golf club properly for two weeks and walked like Marilyn Monroe for the next three weeks.

It was at this house that Mike Yarwood, the impressionist, noticed I spoke with my hands . . . soon after, he flapped them about on a TV special saying, "I wanna tell you a story . . ." Very soon, everybody was doing it, including me. *I walked past a theatre the other day, there was a board outside that said, "£1,000 first prize for the best impersonation of Max Bygraves." Just for a laugh, I went in for it—I came fifth!*

My sister Lily made me laugh more than any comedian. Without trying to be a show-off, she would have a roomful of people convulsed with laughter at the antics we got up to as kids in the Buildings. I was her favourite brother and I loved her as much as she cared for me.

She was a good Catholic but could "Lord Mayor" if she wanted to. She enjoyed almost everything I did so that if a writer gave me a hard time, out would come the stationery and she'd let him or her have it right between the eyes. The one phrase she was fond of was, "If you think it's bloody easy, why not let's see what you can do." I used to tell her not to work herself up, but I think she wrote secretly anyway. She would look after the house at Bournemouth for me, and with her husband Arthur kept the inside and outside like a palace. Then, out of the blue, Arthur, who was the strongest man I've ever known, picked up a virus that was to get steadily worse, so much so, his kidneys failed and he was put on to a dialysis machine. They thought it would be for a few months, instead it turned out to be more than five years.

One morning, I answered a rat-tat on the door. I opened it to find Lily a mixture of excitement and sorrow. She blurted out that she had had a call from the Royal Free Hospital in London to say they had a kidney, taken from a fellow killed in a motor-cycle accident the night before. It was on ice and could be kept for up to four hours. If Arthur could get up there in time, it might do for the transplant he had been in line for.

Lily said she had tried all the taxi services but none was available for the 100-

mile trip to London. I told her not to worry, ran upstairs, got dressed and was set to go in five minutes. Luckily, I had filled the Rolls up the day before, and off we went.

The road was pretty clear. I made Kew Bridge in 90 minutes, almost 100 miles, then came to a roundabout at Chiswick that was chock-a-block, there was a motor-cycle policeman guiding the traffic. I pulled over near him, got out and told him how my passenger had to be at the hospital and there was a deadline. He got out his walkie-talkie and told the story to head-quarters. In six minutes, a police car with two helpful young officers told Arthur to "hop in"; they also advised me not to try and follow as they would probably be breaking some rules. Off they went past the mile or more of stationary vehicles, blue lights flashing and siren going full blast. Arthur said later it was the most exciting day of his life.

At Islington, they had to stop for lights. A pedestrian, a drunken Scotsman, came over to the driver of the police car and, probably looking to be arrested, began to abuse the occupants with the most foul language—calling them Sassenach so and so's, with lots more added. Arthur said the derelict was struck dumb when one of the policemen said, "Hey Jock—why don't you p—off!"

The rush was all in vain, the kidney didn't tally on the computers and Arthur had to go back to the dialysis machine—he spent eight hours every other day on it. Lily never let him get despondent, always with assistance and lots of funny words she worked harder at keeping him happy than anything else. I heard later that several times during his years on the machine he felt like ending it all.

One of Lily's biggest thrills came when I received an invitation to have a private lunch with Her Majesty the Queen and Prince Philip at Buckingham Palace. She tried to take a picture of the embossed invitation with a Marks and Spencer camera; it didn't come out all that well but how she treasured that snapshot.

The invitation came in a roundabout way. I was in my office, the phone rang, I answered. A voice said, "Good morning, I am calling on behalf of Her Majesty to invite you to a private luncheon that the Queen gives periodically for just half a dozen selected guests. Will you be available on the 29th of May?"

I didn't let on that I thought it was Sykes or one of my near pals, so I played along. "Oh, yes," I said, ". . . how lovely —but I would like to know will you have some Spam—and chips, I love chips—and don't forget the treacle pudding." I waited for the laugh—there was none coming. After the pause, the voice said "I'm sure we can find you something you would like."

I suddenly thought, "Hold on, Max," even Mike Yarwood couldn't keep this impression up, this call is for real. I asked him if he was serious. He said, "Most emphatically", then I knew it had to be true because my associates wouldn't know how to say "emphatically". He asked for an address to send the invitation, and next morning it was at my house—brought by the postman, who handed it to me with, "It's from the boss." It didn't have a postage stamp on and when the postman didn't wait for "the posting without a stamp" money, that's when I knew it was genuine.

The distance from my flat to Buckingham Palace is about five hundred yards, so on the great day I flagged a cab and said to the driver, "The Palace, please." He began to head away from Buck House and I asked him where he was going. "Where you said, the Palace." I told him he was going the wrong way, Buckingham Palace was in the opposite direction. "I was taking you to the Palace Theatre—I should have known by the way you're dressed—you look like a poof's butler!" So much for fame.

He dropped me at the gates, the policeman let me through. I walked with hands clasped behind my back in Royal fashion, while hundreds of cameras belonging to overseas visitors clicked away, probably thinking I was something to do with the Royals. I turned round to get the view "they" would get when in residence. There were so many Japanese banging away with their cameras, from where I was standing it looked like a location for *Bridge on the River Kwai*. I was shown into the large banqueting hall to a small picnic-size table that was filled with alcoholic drinks and mixes. I went for a gin and tonic after being turned off a lemonade by the equerry, who said, "Oh, have something stronger." I met my fellow diners, who included Maurice Edelman MP, David, Marquis of Queensberry, Admiral Alexander, Mr. Conway of the Electrical Trades Union and two more whom I can't remember. As I said hello to each of them, I was aware of something going on around my ankles. Looking down I saw two corgis having a nibble at my shoelaces. I bent down, patted them for a few seconds, then stood up to look straight into the eyes of our lovely Queen. "Just knock them away if they're a nuisance," she said. That's how it was, no trumpets —no man in red coat and white gloves shouting "My Lords . . ." After some small talk—into a room the size of a medium suburban dining room, the table set for eight people. The soup, followed by lamb, potatoes and peas with some super wines, was served by smiling gentlemen in olive green livery. The port and brandy was flowing freely. Everything from police pensions to the losses of Concorde were discussed with both the Prince and Her Majesty, proving themselves knowledgeable on all subjects. The luncheon finished at a quarter to three. It must have been enjoyed because we were told it would be through by 2 p.m. or thereabouts. Somebody reminded the Queen she was welcoming the German Ambassador later on. We said our goodbyes and left.

Out on the tarmac, David Queensberry asked me if I would like a lift and I said I would. He directed me to his vehicle, not a Rolls or Daimler, or even a Porsche; it was the dirtiest red Mini. As we drove out of the gates, the guards came to attention, tourists swooped forward to get pictures in case we were "somebody". I sat there thinking, "Please God . . . don't let them recognise me in this heap."

That evening, I had to give a minute-by-minute account to Lily, who lapped up every word. A keen Royalist, she has asked me to repeat the story on many occasions.

Another early morning phone call, and a sobbing Christine, said, "Daddy, some terrible news—we have just gone into Michael's bedroom—he's dead." I didn't know if I was hearing right—not Michael —my first grandson, Michael the practical joker, the one you could get laughing so easily—oh no—he's kidding, he's playing one of his games. He wasn't. Later diagnosed as having legionnaire's disease, he had choked to death in the night.

Christine, who was now happily married to Barry, the artist from Melbourne, was distraught—I'd have given up everything if I could have made her happy but it wasn't to be. They had been living in Hove since returning from Australia so young Mike was buried at the cemetery not too far from their home. It was a bitterly cold day, the mourners were almost frozen. As I walked from the graveside, I saw a figure standing there whom I hardly recognised. White-haired and looking very ill, I saw it was my brother Harry. I went over to him, asked him to come back and have some hot food I had organised at the Norfolk Hotel by Lil and Al Feld. He came, and I was staggered at how ill he looked. Then and there, I told him to get Jean, his wife, forget the pub he was managing and get to my place in the Bahamas. A few days later, they flew off to Nassau. It didn't work, after three days the pain he was suffering was too much so they returned. During this period, I got closer to him than any time during our lives. He always had a rough, tough exterior, but underneath a heart of gold; he never tired of organising charity efforts to help the handicapped and almost everybody without fail adored him, especially his five sons, who were all by now over six feet tall, all except Mick who was the "puzzle"—he was just five feet six inches.

Harry was admitted to the Marsden Hospital in London and lingered for several weeks. In the meantime, I had to take off for another tour of Australia. Soon after arrival, I was playing at a club outside Syndey called Ingleburn. I was putting my jacket on to go on stage when a director of the club came into the room holding a message. "A message from London Max,—your brother died a few hours ago."

Try going out on stage to be funny to a thousand or more people when some idiot, instead of waiting until you came off, tells you as you're going on. I got through the show all right but when I got back into the dressing room, I couldn't hold back the tears. My promoter and friend, Lionel Abrahams, was there to console me and keep visitors out until I recovered. Lionel is such a kindhearted and thoughtful chap, I am eternally grateful to him.

I couldn't get back for the funeral, but pictures backed up the words of an associate: "He must have been the most popular guv'nor in South London". Hundreds attended the burial.

I suppose as you get into the twilight zone, the law of averages makes people you grew up with fade away. Over the last decade, it was happening too much; people of my own age were popping off far too often.

Not too long before Harry left us, I was on my way to Cyril Stapleton's house to rehearse a new *SingalongaMax* album. Just as I was leaving the flat, the phone rang. It was Sheila, Cyril's wife, asking me to come quickly, she thought Cyril was dead in his bed. I rushed to their home near Regent's Park, and it was true—I am not good in a crisis concerning death—I know it is inevitable and that it happens to us all. I comfort as best I can, but to see a lady like Sheila, still with a family, so bewildered, then I don't know how to handle it.

Jock Jacobsen had booked me on a BBC television show called *The Good Old Days*. It was taped from a theatre in Leeds, known as the City of Varieties. It was a good show produced by Barney Colehan, a man responsible for many past successes, including Wilfred Pickles' *Have a Go!* When the show had been recorded, Barney suggested that I use a different route back to London, as there was a big hold-up due to repairs on the motorway.

I took his advice and got hopelessly lost. For some reason, I finished up on the Yorkshire moors. The snow and sleet didn't help conditions, I was thankful the heater and de-misters were working well. At 2.30 a.m. I had no idea where I was. Alone in the car, I pulled into a sheltered spot and spent the night trying to keep warm. To do this, I had to keep starting and stopping the engine to get the heat going. I lay huddled there until the dawn came. When I started the car and drove two or three hundred yards, I saw an inn where I could have stayed and been warm and comfortable. I stopped and went in to ask the way to London; the helpful people directed me, then ten miles later, the car stalled—oh no, out of petrol.

By the time I rectified the fuel problem it was past 10 a.m. but at last I was on the road to London. At the wheel, I was practising some of the names I was going to call Jock for booking me in mid-winter on a show up north, without a driver, for a meagre BBC fee. As I drove down Park Lane in London, I remembered how hungry I was. I swung the car into Curzon Street and parked outside the 21 Club.

When Harry Meadows, the owner of the club, saw me he said I looked like death. I had a wash and brush up in Harry's apartment. In the meantime, Harry had ordered me eggs, bacon, sausage and mushrooms which I began to tuck into. In the middle of this, I was told there was a telephone call for me. Strange, I didn't even know I was coming to the 21 myself —how did anybody else? The call was from Sydney, Australia, with a heart-broken Lionel Abrahams on the other end, saying how sad he was to hear the news.

"What news?" I told him I had been away and hadn't heard any bad news, what was it? "Jock died in the night—heart attack." Lovely, gentle Jock, my manager and adviser, had passed on. After almost thirty years' partnership without a contract, only trust in each other, Jock was no more. I miss him to this day and have never used another personal agent since he went in 1977. I still can't get over the fact that I heard the news from my promoter in Sydney, yet our office was only a stride away from the 21.

Then lots of pals I had worked and laughed and dined with, were going fast. Blossom and I were watching Tommy Cooper one Sunday on *Live from Her Majesty's* TV show. Suddenly I saw him fall to the ground—the audience laughed —the curtains closed with no play-off into the commercial. I told my wife that something was amiss—I had known Tommy for many years and knew he never never did "falling down" gags. The week after, we were attending his funeral at Mortlake Crematorium. On that day, commiserating with Eric Morecambe and Dickie Henderson, we said our goodbyes. I didn't dream when I left both those two great blokes that it would be the finale for them too. When I asked Dickie on the phone if he would like me to come and see him, he said, "Please don't, Max—I'm not a pretty sight." Dickie died shortly after—another terrible shock.

Then came the death of Norrie Paramor, the man who had succeeded Cyril Stapleton at Pye Records—a great musician and, like Cyril, a gentleman in every sense of the word, they both were *gentle* men. Joan, his lovely wife, broke the news to me—Cyril and Norrie are sadly missed. The highest tribute I can pay them both is that during their life-span with their music, they made millions happy, they don't come much better than Cyril and Norrie and each time I hear a singalong record that either one of them produced, I get a warm glow from their expertise and guidance.

Arthur, my brother-in-law, in the meantime had been fitted with a new kidney and become a new man. Lily, after nursing him for five years or more, said at last she could relax. I went up to Nottingham to record some shows for *Family Fortunes*. At the hotel one evening, Blossom phoned to say Lily had gone into hospital with stomach pains a few days previously. "Is it serious?" I asked. Bloss said she didn't know. Bloss loved Lily even more than me, if that's possible.

I told her I would call a top specialist I knew at Poole Hospital and perhaps he could give me some news. The top man there was Doctor Ronnie Fisher—I had done some fund-raising for Ronnie's Cancer Research in the past and asked his help to find out what was wrong with my sister. He was most obliging, said he would call me back. I was just leaving for the studio to record the shows when the phone rang. Once again, I couldn't believe what I was hearing. Lily had only been in a couple of days and Ronnie was saying things like, "Sorry—no hope—we'll try chemotherapy—wish I had better news . . ."

Oh, our lovely Lily, so full of fun, so

good to everybody—so happy that her beloved Arthur was all right. She requested the Last Rites and was at peace to go to meet her Maker. When I am in Bournemouth, I have to drive past the road she lived in. Frequently, I find myself looking for her walking back from the shops. When she was alive and I came along in the car, I'd toot the horn—she'd get in, laughing helplessly at the idea of this housewife with her shopping bag riding home in a Rolls.

Another favourite line of hers, remembering our childhood days, happened when somebody asked her if she knew Max Bygraves. She'd say, "Know him? I slept with him for years."

Then it was the turn of another Lily to go. My mother, at eighty-six, said she'd had a wonderful innings, having six children, nineteen grandchildren and eighteen great-grandchildren. This lady had been a great battler; never once did I hear her complain in a whole lifetime. When I went in with our large family to see her at Greenwich Hospital where she died, the sister had to ask the visitors to slow down, there were too many of us in the ward. She died smiling at quite a lot of the family she had started.

At the burial, the most amazing thing happened. Her burial plot was below a cherry tree alongside my father's. As the priest waited for the last mourner to arrive, the birds in the tree twittered so loudly it was impossible to hear another sound—the priest raised his prayer book to begin his Requiem—the dozens and dozens of birds cut out totally.

The priest said the beautiful words, and as he pronounced "Amen", the whole gang of robins and starlings began again, it was if they had been cued.

Lily—my mother, had gone.

It was a great personal pleasure to me when Anthony and Celia, his wife, named their first daughter—Lily.

As I write this particular part of the book, I am overlooking Sydney Harbour. It is a tranquil night, ferries are steaming lazily from the North Shore to the South, it is 32° (about 90° Farenheit). I have just put the phone down having learned from London that Frank Barber, the man who was responsible for the orchestrations I have used over the years, has passed away. Goodbye Frank and thanks for all those wonderful musical notes you put down to make people like myself sound so much more acceptable.

I think I'll put the pen away, go to bed and think about some of the lovely people I have mentioned—think of how lucky I am to have known them.

20

ANTHONY married Celia on New Year's Eve 1981 at our house in the Bahamas. The Negro preacher gave them his blessing, then we sat down to a wedding breakfast in the garden. After a bright sunny morning, clouds gathered, the wind rose to hurricane force, the guests had to leave the garden where the chairs and tables were arranged for the wedding breakfast, to take shelter inside. It was panic stations as we tried to rearrange the seating for more than one hundred people. Blossom's WAAF training came to the fore as she instructed the men to carry out settees and armchairs to replace them with trestle tables and folding chairs.

Filled with champagne, the guests happily complied with the instructions. It was as if Pickford's had arrived. Had it been in Rotherhithe, neighbours would have thought we were being evicted. It is the sort of scene that is described each time a family gets together to reminisce.

Before the year was out, Lily was born. When Celia pulled back the shawl to reveal the one-day-old babe, it was all I could do to hold back the tears of joy. The following year another one came, this time named Tallulah, who has grown to be a real little madam.

A couple of months ago, as I was ribbing her as she was painting in her colouring book she pointed the paintbrush at me, then said, "Look—I happen to be in a good mood—so stop teasing me." It's a long time since I was reprimanded by a four year old—she has the makings of a Prime Minister—I hope she'll be happy at Number Ten.

The following year, another one. This time a boy, to be named Ashley. They are living at present in Malta and on the visit when Tallulah was doing her impression of Bette Davis, Ashley was showing me his impersonation of a punk rocker. He came up to me as I sat in the armchair—smiled—then kicked me in the shins—hard. When I tried to pretend it didn't hurt he did it again. I pointed behind him and said, "Oh look—a rabbit." When he turned to look, I kicked him up the arse. He has left my shins alone since.

Shortly after the marriage of Celia and Anthony, another wedding. This time my youngest daughter Maxine, to Barry, a young man from North Wales. Barry speaks and teaches Spanish, and after trying a couple of years to face English winters, they gave up and moved to Spain with their newborn baby Oscar. The exact opposite of Ashley, Oscar likes to find out what makes life tick. As I have spent much longer with Oscar, he will listen to any "story" I tell him, especially if it is a "made up" one; he prefers those to being read to. I like it too because I can let my imagination run wild.

He is now four; my daughter, who was pregnant again, asked Oscar if it was a baby brother what would he like to call him. Oscar replied, "Barnaby". The name appealed to Barry and Maxine. When the baby was born it was indeed a boy, who was christened Barnaby.

One morning I took Oscar for a walk along a sunny Spanish country lane. I asked what made him choose the name of

Barnaby for his new brother. "It's the name of the chicken in *Sesame Street*," he replied. I haven't got round to mentioning it to Granma Blossom yet.

My pal Sykes is a hard-working creative writer who, more as a means of making a living, turned to performing. He made a huge success of it. Writing is a badly paid means of making a crust so Eric worked on his talent of script reading, then, slowly but surely, made his way into television. His series with Hattie Jaques ran for sixteen years on BBC and endeared both of them to the British public. From these shows, he graduated to farce, first with Jimmy Edwards in *Big Bad Mouse*, then to various Whitehall and Ray Cooney hits —there isn't a funnier exponent of the game in Britain today. All this achieved with a hearing problem that would have made most men turn to other work. We have never had an argument in forty years —until last year.

Eric was appearing in my home town of Bournemouth with the show *Run for your Wife*, a winner of an idea that starred Eric,

Terry Scott and some very competent supporting actors and actresses.

We were in the middle of a golf game when Eric, who was not playing too well, complained of feeling tired. I happened to be on form this day, five holes ahead, which was not usual because when Eric is on top form, he is hard to beat. He sighed, then said, "It's all right for you—you walk on the stage, sing a few songs, then the audience does the work, I have it different."

I blew up. "What d'ye mean, for Chrissake—I don't have the safety of a book show with all the laughs mapped out along the way, I am on that bloody stage for one and a half hours feeding myself lines—I don't have actors around me setting the laughs up—I don't have time to coast—if there is a three-second hold up, I have to cover it. Furthermore, I can't go into the dressing room for a ten-minute smoke while the plot is kept going by the supporting cast—I have to be as fit and quick as a boxer to deliver lines for ninety minutes. If you think audiences stand for me letting them do the work, you've got it all wrong—perhaps for five minutes they'll join in, the rest of the time *I* am bloody well entertaining them!!!"

Eric stood open-mouthed, then broke into a grin. "That's the first time in forty years I've ever heard you do your nut . . ." He shook with laughter, ". . . your face went real pointed." We both finished up laughing at my indignation, it made not one iota of difference to our friendship.

It is a fact though that stand-up comedy is the toughest form of show business there is. I think the two worst forms of suicide are pouring petrol over yourself and adding a match, the second is becoming a stand-up comedian. I don't mean the comic that goes around stealing jokes from other comedians, the one who holds a microphone with one hand, leans on the stand with the other, then says, "Did you hear the one about the Irishman . . ." I mean the fellow who has got an original comedy angle and works on persona—the lad that makes himself become more important than his material. On entering the business, working to audiences, he is going to know some of the loneliest days and nights ever, he will hear silences that he thought only belonged to a church, he will walk the streets trying to fill in that quietness because a stand-up comic doesn't hear laughter—he hears the silence. His waking hours will be filled by wondering how to plug the void. When he does get on top of it, he will walk out of the venue he is working and his feet will hardly touch the ground.

Once, during an interview with a prominent writer, I was asked if the film I was making seemed like hard work; when I told the lady writer I found it easy compared with stage work, she was surprised.

It was hard to explain that like the farces Eric was in, other actors kept the plot going, you were allowed to muck up your lines and "take" another ten or twenty times to get it right—the lighting was arranged to make you look good—the sound always worked—on top of all this, lackeys brought you tea or coffee and attended to every whim. All you really needed was a face that suited the part and a decent memory for dialogue.

There's hardly a branch of the entertainment business I haven't tried—the stand-up act is the toughest—probably why there are so few in the world attempting it nowadays; it's easier to learn three chords on a guitar and get the engineer to "up" the volume when a wrong note is played.

During the late Forties when almost every rookie that had performed in a Forces concert decided to "have a go", there was a lot of original talent around, but many did not make it through no fault of their own. A stand-up comic at that time named Frank Harris, who should have been a star but didn't make it because of health reasons, was on the same bill as myself. We were due to appear on John Sharman's *Music Hall*; this was a BBC radio show with a twenty million listening audience. The orchestra leader was Rae Jenkins, a superb conductor and a helpful gentleman.

Frank, who had little knowledge of the workings of broadcasting, had been told to bring his play-on music. He turned up with a sixpenny piano copy of "Happy Days are Here Again", which he handed to Rae Jenkins.

"What's this?" asked Mr. Jenkins.

Frank told him it was his play-on music. "But I've got thirty-two men in the orchestra and they all need a copy." Without batting an eyelid, Harris said, "Well, can't they crowd round?" *That* was the sort of confidence needed to be a stand-up comic.

21

ACALL from the War Office. Would I fly over to Germany to entertain troops stationed in West Berlin and open a fête for the wives and children on a Saturday afternoon? I agreed, but didn't feel too enamoured with the idea. I guessed it would be an engagement that would have me performing in some all-purpose gymnasium that had inadequate lighting, a bad sound system and an audience of raucous Servicemen. I couldn't have been more wrong.

On arrival in Berlin, a Guards captain greeted Blossom and me at the steps of the British Airways plane. A staff car arrived, driven by a female corporal from Bournemouth who could have graced the cover of a glossy magazine.

We were driven to Brigadier Evans's home, where outside four German soldiers patrolled with Sten guns at the ready, twenty-four hours a day.

Mrs. Shirley Evans (known among the

men as Shirl the Whirl), made us so comfortable in their home, it was easy to see the four days there were going to be a delight. After a most enjoyable dinner with the Brigadier, followed by cigars and brandy, we retired to the most comfortable bed I have ever slept in.

Next day, we were handed a sheet that had every minute itemised for the next three days. Early morning was a trip through Checkpoint Charlie into the Russian sector, where *four* Irish coffees came to less than one pound. The drive, which was meant to be a sightseeing tour, took us round the old Germany that once took in Nuremberg and buildings that had been fought for by Russian troops not all that long ago. We watched goose-stepping soldiers changing guard quite near to a hill where it was reckoned 20,000 Russian troops had been buried. Suddenly, although it was 1985, the war I had been a Serviceman in, seemed as if it had been over only a few days, yet here Blossom and I were watching ourselves reflected in the young soldiers and WAAC girls as if we were part of it. It was hard to think of ourselves as grandparents, standing there hoping that nothing like it ever happened again.

The following day, a drive around West Berlin. The officer explained that next week he would be in Spandau Prison guarding the Nazi Rudolf Hess who was still alive at that time. When I asked him to tell me more about Hess as a prisoner, he ventured that Hess liked the British as guards, he read and wrote all day in a most contented fashion, but when it was the turn of the Russians to guard him, he invariably lost weight and had to have constant medication.

It was probably the most comic prison in history. Four different army sections taking turns to watch over a man in his nineties—talk about a political ploy— some day somebody is going to write a great comedy about it—I wish I knew how, I'll bet it would be a bigger success than Mel Brooks's *The Producers*.

Later in the day, we were taken into the arena where Adolf Hitler watched coloured runner Jesse Owens break the Olympic record and refused to acknowledge the Negro's effort. Surprise, surprise, Blossom and I were the guests of honour as three different regimental bands all came marching towards us with the troops in full marching order, swinging their way to the podium we were seated on. Three bands played a special arrangement of my composition "You Need Hands", followed by "Tulips from Amsterdam". I laugh now but at the time it was the proudest moment I have ever known.

After that, a walk round the stalls, shaking hands with the wives of Servicemen, who were selling cakes and pastries, home-made jams, knitted sweaters and so on to raise money for the Benevolent Fund. As a finale, paratroopers dropped from the sky and landed a few feet from us with flowers for Blossom and, for me, an embroidered crest of three regiments that must have taken many hours to complete. I keep it at home and feel a glow each time I look at it on the wall.

After I had performed for the troops and their families in most favourable circumstances, a well-equipped theatre with plush seating, good lighting and sound, we finished the day exhausted and slept like tops.

The next day was Sunday. As we

weren't flying back to London until the evening, a staff car was sent to take us for a tour of the British sector. It was a warm sunny day, the Berliners were out in force. As we cruised along the parkside, Blossom suddenly exclaimed, "I just saw a man with no clothes on!" I told her she probably saw a fellow with a flesh-coloured pair of swim trunks that made him look as if he was nude. Neither the Captain nor the corporal driver said anything—they just smiled quietly. We stopped in the park and we were invited to stretch our legs. We ambled down to the river edge to admire the ducks and swans. Suddenly, from Bloss, "Oh my God!". Sure enough, she had been right, walking towards us were two "gentlemen" in their thirties— stark naked! Two more, not a stitch on, were reading Sunday papers as kids on skateboards and cycles went by obliviously. Looking round, there were dozens of them—naked men and strollers fully clothed in the latest fashions—somehow, the two didn't go together. With that German stance of hands clasped behind their backs, heads erect, defying the stares of the uninitiated, it brought another

Blossom gem later when she related the episode to the family back in England. "You should have seen them—they were as naked as the day they were born—and twice as cocky!"

The OBE stands for Order of the British Empire. On the day of the investiture, recipients arrive at Buckingham Palace with their families and friends, to witness what must be one of the finest stage-managed events, but taken in its stride by the hardworking and knowledgeable team at the home of the Queen.

For many of these families, seeing it for the first time, the sight is awe-inspiring. I took the three ladies in our family along—Blossom and my two daughters, Christine and Maxine. I would liked to have had Anthony present but his wife Celia was busy having babies at that time. *Three children under three—I said to Anthony, "I'd like to take you to the zoo—let the rabbits have a look at you."*

As the guests tread the red carpet to the Ballroom, they pass HM. Life Guards with swords raised, standing unblinkingly like some giant Ronson lighter. The guests make their way to seats arranged to face Her Majesty and the receivers of the awards. In a gallery, a band of the Guards plays—no brass or woodwind, just strings. I was told the presentations would begin at 10 a.m. and should finish at midday.

I stood next to Willie Carson, the jockey —I was the last of the Bs, Willie was first of the Cs. As you reach the Queen, your name is whispered to her—she has a few words, then pins the medal of the OBE on your lapel. She is such a fine-looking lady, very few photographs capture the softness of her eyes, the smile that plays around the corners of her mouth, the texture of her skin and the pleasure she seems to exude from doing a job that, if not tiresome, must be repetitive.

I somehow felt that I wasn't entitled to be there because I was being rewarded for a job that I have found easy and enjoyable. If I have helped to raise money for charity, it has all come about by my love of the game. I felt very humble as I rubbed shoulders with voluntary workers who dedicate most of their spare time to helping others who can't help themselves, surgeons who have saved lives, scientists whose dedication has helped to make life easier for many, even humble tea-ladies who served the nectar to Civil Servants for forty-odd years.

As I reached the rostrum, the band struck up "Maybe It's Because I'm a Londoner". I felt like going into a soft-shoe chorus. Then, as the very last recipient received the award, Big Ben struck the hour of twelve, we rose from our seats, Her Majesty smiled a radiant smile at all, then departed. To me, it was stage management at its best. Let the anti-Royalists take a jump—God Save the Queen!

one through yet, so maybe the audience sensed that distaste. The funny thing about that show is that I put it back into the ratings; most viewers found the approach I used okay. I actually could look at contestants' faces and sense the turmoil going on inside them, that made me want to linger and help the players, perhaps that's what some viewers found lethargic. Out of it came the catchphrase "Big Money" but, professionally, it didn't help my television career, it helped buy another jet fighter plane for the RAF from the tax on the fee I received, but with hindsight, I don't think it was a wise decision.

I suppose there are more chances of meeting doubtful characters in our business than the Stock Exchange. At the moment, there is a fellow in Canada who is selling our albums in most English-speaking countries. I know him, he was introduced to me by the British record company. I made a commercial for him which he took to Toronto without paying any of the technicians. I know for a fact he has been paid handsomely by a record company in Australia, his sales in US and Canada are big, yet the London company have received little in the way of royalties compared with the sales he has marked up. I had to make a fuss and, eventually, London decided to get a lawyer on to him. The lawyer will probably make a lot more than we do.

In Hong Kong, there is another dealer who copies and presses records from an ordinary LP, then sells them at cut price all over Asia. My sales are negligible, but I have seen the palace this fellow lives in, all from sales of Michael Jackson, Bruce Springsteen and whoever is currently in the Top Ten. The trade is trying to clamp down because millions are lost annually through this system, what the pirates laughingly call "a record turnover". *You must believe me—I walked through a market-place in Calcutta more than eighteen years ago and saw an armless beggar with a portable gramophone, which he wound up with his mouth, playing— believe me—my record of "You Need Hands"—this is not a joke.*

This *is* a joke, but it was on me. Staying at the apartments I have stayed at for the past twenty-four years on Sydney Harbour, was lovely Ronnie Corbett with his gorgeous wife Anne. Ronnie had his car stolen after stopping for a meal in the notorious district of King's Cross—equal to London's Soho. He not only made the press in Australia, they used the story in most of the dailies in the UK. Ronnie was on the way home from a show and most of his props were in the boot—suit, shoes, shirts, etc. A reporter from the *Telegraph*, a local scribe, got on the phone to me by mistake; he thought he was talking to Ronnie. "What did you lose?" he asked. I replied, "Everything—suit, socks, shirts —*stilts* . . ." He loved that, so did Ronnie when the article came out next day.

On that day, I took my wife to town, parked on a meter near Sydney's Hyde Park, then shopped for a couple of hours at the David Jones store. When we returned to the car it was gone. I thought, I can't say it was stolen, not after Ronnie's car was pinched twenty-four hours earlier, people will think I'm getting on Ronnie's bandwagon. I went back to David Jones, phoned Lionel's office and told him the car had been nicked.

He told me to sit tight, he would send his car for me, meanwhile, he'd report the theft to Hertz and the police. We sat there for fifteen minutes, then Lionel himself turned up in his Rolls-Royce to take me back home. I told him on the way that Sydney could do with a smarter police force—two cars stolen in two days was a bad record. As we glided up William Street, I couldn't believe what I saw; there was my car on another parking meter. We were on a main road, I told Lionel to pull over, there were dozens of cars behind us, I called, "Go on—I'll see you back at your office!" Off he went with Blossom, the cars behind giving him a hard time with their horns. I still don't know whether I got the meter I was parked on mixed up, or whether it had really been stolen and put back on a different meter. I got in and drove off. The journey back to my apartment is about three miles from city centre. Half-way there, in the rear view mirror, I noticed a police car trailing me. I kept an eye on the speedometer and kept to the inside lane—so did the police car. When I pulled up outside my flat, the police car stopped too.

In true *Miami Vice* style, out stepped two policemen, both unbuttoning their revolvers, and walked up to me. "Can I see your driving licence sir?" I didn't have it with me, I told them so. "Can I have your name, sir?" Usually, in Sydney, a few people know the name of Max Bygraves, but these two herberts showed no recognition. "Have you been drinking sir?" I asked them what gave them that idea, they said again, "Can we have your *real* name sir?" I told them it was my real name, then one said, "You are driving a stolen vehicle." I remembered my wife was waiting for me at Lionel's office so I said to the police officers, "I can prove who I am, if you will let me go up to my flat—my licence is up there." The officer felt for his handcuffs saying, "We'd rather you came with us—you can explain everything there."

One officer took away the keys of the Hertz hire car, I was told to climb into the back seat, they drove off towards the city but cut down to Double Bay and finally stopped outside Lionel's office. They walked me inside saying on the way that if the gentleman who filed the report recognised me, everything would be okay. I was led into Lionel's plush office where he sat with Blossom convulsed with laughter—both of them. They'd set me up!

On the way back in the Rolls, Lionel had used the car phone to outline to the sergeant he knew at the station, that he'd seen the car on William Street with somebody who wasn't Max Bygraves driving it. This Lionel had engineered to get his own back on a gag I had pulled on him in Brisbane. That was the time I walked into his suite at the hotel where we were staying—he had just got out of the shower when his phone rang; as he answered he asked me to pass the deodorant aerosol—I passed him the hairspray—he had to take another shower.

23

I LEFT Australia two days ago. We are now in the Hyatt Hotel, Hong Kong, watching the news on television. It is dominated by a team of highjackers that have taken a Kuwaiti airliner, they are holding fifty hostages. Two of the hostages have been murdered and their bodies thrown from the aeroplane on to the tarmac at Cyprus.

I couldn't help thinking that in this day and age of sending men and missiles to the moon, some boffin hasn't come up with an idea that as soon as a pilot knows he is to be hijacked and landed his plane, a harmless gas is triggered off that sends passengers and hijackers to sleep in seconds. The authorities now board the plane, arrest the hijackers and allow the passengers to wake up in their own time. The more I think about it, the more feasible it seems. There must be arguments against it, but it wouldn't stop us accepting it from some Hollywood movie.

I have been in Hong Kong several times. In the old days I played The Button, which at one time was atop the famous Mandarin Hotel. For weeks I stayed on the island of Hong Kong, now I find that part most dreary—I stay on the opposite side, Kowloon, where recently I appeared at the Pink Giraffe, a supper club on top of the Sheraton Hotel.

Kowloon doesn't get going until late evening, then, you can find any sort of entertainment your heart desires. One place, known as Bottoms Up is where tourists sit round a circular bar and chat to the topless waitresses and barmaids. It is run by a friend of ours named Patricia Sephton. In the war days, Pat worked at the Windmill Theatre when "it never closed". Later, she came to Hong Kong with her husband Vic, a bass player with the Keymen, now she keeps the Bottoms Up—up. *Vic said, "Come with me, I'll take you to a topless restaurant"—we walked for half an hour to this café that didn't have a roof on.*

Pat talked me into visiting the BU a few years back; it was their first birthday. I went quite innocently. I was asked to cut the birthday cake. As I put the knife into the cake, two naked employees with the biggest boobs you've ever seen appeared from nowhere and stood beside me. At the same time, up came Vic with his Leica, said, "Smile" and that flipping picture is still in the frame outside the place. No amount of asking Pat to take it down has worked. Many people come up to me in the UK and say, "I saw your picture outside a porno place in Hong Kong!" Bloss, who was with me at the time and saw me "set up", hurries like mad when we go past the BU; it is just a few steps away from the hotel where we are staying. For a game, I drag back and say, "Hold on, Bloss—let's see if I am still in vogue!" She pulls me by the arm saying, "Come on—you dirty old man."

It is well known that Hong Kong is the place to go for "replicas". They can pass off a Dunhill Pen, a Gucci belt, a Cartier watch or whatever for almost nothing. Strolling down Nathan Road in Kowloon last evening, we were pounced on by a youth with big smile and darting eyes. "Want a Rolex watch?" he inquired. Now a Rolex watch of the type he flashed would cost upwards of £3,000, this one he was offering for £15. "Why don't you get one just for a laugh," said Bloss. "It might make an interesting page in your book." I was reluctant but she pulled my arm. "Go on—he's got such a nice face." This, from the lady who makes excuses for Hitler. I tried to keep walking, which is not easy to do on crowded Nathan Road in the evening.

She won; we walked back to the young man who saw we were interested. Instead of selling me the watch there and then, he beckoned us to follow him. From the crowded road, we followed him to an alley, up a rickety flight of stairs, where natives sat on their haunches smoking—I have been in rooms where the smell of marijuana stays with you—this lot were smoking the same. We walked across extended legs to a room with a fluorescent strip; in the corner a man slept on a bunk, at a table sat a Chinese gentleman with a jeweller's glass in his eye working at some cheap jewellery. The boy was still smiling. Bloss thought it was *so* exciting. I was expecting to be mugged at any moment. He spread out a dozen or more Rolex replicas, then asked me to make my selection. All I wanted to do was get back on to Nathan Road again. I pointed to one, got the two hundred Hong Kong dollars ready and made to leave. This didn't please the youth, he wanted to demonstrate the workings of the Rolex, how to change the date, wind on, etc. All the time, I had one eye cocked in case I was "jumped". Blossom was oblivious to it all.

The next day, in the *China Daily Mail*, was a front page picture of a steamroller about to run over hundreds and hundreds of counterfeit watches that had been unearthed by the Hong Kong police. A few days later, as we passed through Customs at Heathrow, I was asked if I had anything to declare. I told the Customs officer I had a Rolex watch. He asked to see it. I showed him. "How much did you pay for this, sir?" I told him it was a bargain and that all I gave for it was £3,500. He gave me a pitying look, after examining it once more. I asked him if he liked it and he replied with a smile, "It should give you many *minutes* of pleasure." Up till now, it still goes.

24

FOR the past ten weeks, I have bedded down at hotels as far apart as San Francisco—Tahiti—Hong Kong—Auckland—Bangkok—Perth—and back home here in London. The weather during that time has left a lot to be desired. Floods in Queensland, devastation in New Zealand, torrential rain in Tasmania, fog in LA—in fact, the one place that seems to have had the best of the elements has been the little old British Isles.

Of course, I could never have got down to writing these afterthoughts had I stayed in the UK, so Blossom's suggestion to take some writing material along was a good one. Now, back in London Town, it is a question of getting these pages assembled and off to the publishers. Hopefully, they will believe there is entertainment among them. If they give a smile along the way, what I set out to achieve may have happened. There seemed so much to write about that had to be left out. I would like to have written more about Bob Dixon, a character, he has accompanied me on piano for every engagement (except one, when his dear old mum died) for the past thirty-five years—never practises, yet each performance plays as though it's the first time, so keen he is to please.

I could have found a page or two for Wally Thompson, who joined me fifteen years ago when the Billy Cotton Band broke up. He was the drummer with Bill's band. He boasts that the reason he holds this job with me is, not because he is a good drummer (which he is), but because he has a loud laugh that triggers my audience. He has heard me refer to him as Cymbal Simon for the past ten years but still guffaws as if it were a new ad lib.

You cannot write at length about a life or career without mentioning people who have helped along the way. Let me take a line to mention Bert Mortimer, my "Man Friday", which is too simple a word for a gentleman who looks after my wardrobe, laundry, travel, make-up and so on. Not only that, he looks after Wally and Bob like a father. Bert was employed by Peter Sellers doing much the same as he does for me; he worked for Peter for sixteen years. He joined me eight years ago and his smiling countenance makes him a pleasure to have around. Believe me, when a team works as closely as we do, there is no room for glumness, sulking or bad feeling. Good feeling isn't found overnight, it has to mature and I am thankful that these three men came along to help my efforts.

Lastly, there is Jennifer, my secretary confidentiale. Jennifer has had only this one job since she left her college. For the past twenty-four years, this personable, attractive lady, who is a joy to have working so diligently, is hardly ever without a smile. Married to naturalised Italian Paul, she lights up the office and handles the business affairs so competently that I am reluctant to purchase a computer. When I travel abroad, Jennifer stays behind to man the office—I am in touch with her each day by phone from whichever part of the world I am in. I can tell what the weather is like in London by the way she answers the call. "Good morning—Max Bygraves' office" means bright sunshine, plain "Hello" means thundery showers, a sharp intake of air, followed by "MB Limited" means, "I've got a cold—keep it short!" She is a gem.

I would like to have elaborated on the time I wrote to Mrs. Thatcher with an idea to cut down unemployment in Britain—land of my birth and land that I love. The idea was to have something in the UK similar to the 1800 clubs they have in New South Wales. These clubs are social places for the men and women who like an evening's chat—cheap good meal—drinks at almost half pub prices, with entertainment that costs just a few pence a week. To make this work for the members (one club alone has over fifty thousand of them), they have poker machines. The profit made must be ploughed back in to the clubs so it is almost a case of the wealthy subsidizing the not so well off. Tax is paid on all these machines from which the NSW government takes millions of dollars. On top of this, employment is found for large staffs —administration—waiters—musicians— carpenters—carpet-makers—carpet layers

—plumbers—you name a trade, the clubs seem to use almost every profession.

I had a courteous reply from Downing Street telling me that the Prime Minister was interested and would be looking into it. When I heard nothing for almost a year, I wrote again as a reminder. This time, I got a curt reply with the message ". . . the Prime Minister has said all she wishes to say on this subject . . ."

Well, that was a great source of revenue thrown out by a government that could have had several more millions to give the aged and the rest of the country that suffers because of lack of funds. I would like to mention that NSW in Australia enjoys the greatest standard of living in the world.

Politics? I am not all that keen on them— no matter who you vote for, a politician always gets in. I am still trying to work out why Lord Wilson said "goodbye" when he did, why we were suddenly given a Prime Minister who had been no great shakes as Foreign Minister, was responsible for putting the troops into Northern Ireland when Home Secretary and as Chancellor of the Exchequer devalued the pound. After Harold made his exit, the British public suddenly became aware they had a PM that nobody voted for. I wish Lord Callaghan long life and happiness, but I would still like to know how it was done.

I would also like to have written at length about the gentleman from Barnstaple in north Devon, who wrote to me after I had made a television appeal on behalf of Cancer Research—and told me I was wasting my time. I thought at first he was some kind of crank; we get some unbelievable correspondence from listeners and viewers after an appearance, some you read, others go straight in the waste bin, but this chap made sense.

Briefly, he told me that even though the Research had gathered many millions from donations, the advance towards a remedy was practically nothing. He advocated there was a nature cure available to practically everybody that wanted to try, called the Grape Cure. He sent a copy of a book that was printed in Pietermaritzberg, South Africa written by Professor Joanna Brandt. The theory that Joanna Brandt had explored was that the grape contains enough vitamins and sustenance to feed the body for at least three months. Grapes contain sugar—yet, if left, is the only fruit that will not rot—it will turn to a raisin— eat the pips and they provide "roughage".

When one thinks that from time's beginning, grapes have been the food brought to invalids in hospitals—how Romans treated most ills with them, there must be an element of truth. Brandt proved that by eating only grapes for a long period, the blood was purified. Suffering from cancer —arthritis and many more complaints, is either cured or relieved without drugs.

It would take another book to tell of the people I have mentioned the Grape Cure to who feel better for it. I know this, should I ever feel I was ailing, I would go for this "nothing to lose" theory. Even without ailments, it was the correspondence that convinced me I should eat at least a couple of pounds of grapes a week—and I feel absolutely A1 at the moment.

I once asked two prominent doctors if there was any truth in Professor Brandt's findings; they replied, "Of course there is

—but don't tell too many people—otherwise you'll put us all out of work."

A rule of the comedy business is, "Never leave the stage without a laugh." The reason for this is that if you don't cover your exit with laughter, it means walking off stage to the sound of your own footsteps—a sound that makes most funny men shudder. So, with the winding up of this epistle, "I Wanna Tell You a Story" . . . a tale that makes me laugh each time I remember it.

A small party of entertainers was invited to Kenya in East Africa for a golfing expedition to raise funds for local charities. Among the travellers were Henry Cooper, Eric Sykes, and Dickie Henderson. It is hard to believe that Henry, who was just a bell away from being heavyweight champion of the world, should be afraid of anything, but he was at that time, he was very timid about, of all things—flying!

On a beautiful African day, the party was invited to visit an African village some fifty miles away. Arriving at the airfield, they saw the aeroplane that was to take them there. It was a fabric-covered relic from the Second World War that had been used for ferrying paratroopers. The pilot, who wore glasses with lenses like the bottom of jam-jars, inspired no confidence. It was all they could do to stop Henry running off there and then.

As the two engines spluttered into life, Henry gripped the arms of the makeshift seats until those famous knuckles showed white. He sat there, eyes closed, lips moving silently in prayer, from a take-off to a landing that would have done credit to a Hell's Angels movie.

The guide showed them round the native village with Henry trying to listen but still thinking of the return flight. "Every building you see here . . ." said the guide, "is made from dung, the walls are dung—dung that is dried and moulded to the shapes you see . . ."

At this, Sykes piped up with, "You should have been sitting next to Henry on the plane this morning—you'd have got yourself a new town hall!"

B-boom!

GUIDE
TO THE COLOUR CODING
OF
ULVERSCROFT BOOKS

Many of our readers have written to us expressing their appreciation for the way in which our colour coding has assisted them in selecting the Ulverscroft books of their choice. To remind everyone of our colour coding—this is as follows:

BLACK COVERS
Mysteries

★

BLUE COVERS
Romances

★

RED COVERS
Adventure Suspense and General Fiction

★

ORANGE COVERS
Westerns

★

GREEN COVERS
Non-Fiction

NON-FICTION TITLES
in the
Ulverscroft Large Print Series

No Time for Romance	*Lucilla Andrews*
Life's A Jubilee	*Maud Anson*
Beautiful Just! and	
Bruach Blend	*Lillian Beckwith*
An Autobiography Vol.1	
Vol.2	*Agatha Christie*
Just Here, Doctor	*Robert D. Clifford*
High Hopes	*Norman Croucher*
An Open Book	*Monica Dickens*
Going West with Annabelle	*Molly Douglas*
The Drunken Forest	*Gerald Durrell*
The Garden of the Gods	*Gerald Durrell*
Golden Bats and Pink Pigeons	*Gerald Durrell*
If Only They Could Talk	*James Herriot*
It Shouldn't Happen to a Vet	*James Herriot*
Let Sleeping Vets Lie	*James Herriot*
Vet in a Spin	*James Herriot*
Vet in Harness	*James Herriot*
Vets Might Fly	*James Herriot*
Emma and I	*Sheila Hocken*
White Man Returns	*Agnes Newton Keith*
Flying Nurse	*Robin Miller*
The High Girders	*John Prebble*
The Seventh Commandment	*Sarah Shears*
Zoo Vet	*David Taylor*

FICTION TITLES
in the
Ulverscroft Large Print Series

The Onedin Line: The High Seas
                              Cyril Abraham
The Onedin Line: The Iron Ships
                              Cyril Abraham
The Onedin Line: The Shipmaster
                              Cyril Abraham
The Onedin Line: The Trade Winds
                              Cyril Abraham
The Enemy   *Desmond Bagley*
Flyaway   *Desmond Bagley*
The Master Idol   *Anthony Burton*
The Navigators   *Anthony Burton*
A Place to Stand   *Anthony Burton*
The Doomsday Carrier   *Victor Canning*
The Cinder Path   *Catherine Cookson*
The Girl   *Catherine Cookson*
The Invisible Cord   *Catherine Cookson*
Life and Mary Ann   *Catherine Cookson*
Maggie Rowan   *Catherine Cookson*
Marriage and Mary Ann   *Catherine Cookson*
Mary Ann's Angels   *Catherine Cookson*
All Over the Town   *R. F. Delderfield*
Jamaica Inn   *Daphne du Maurier*
My Cousin Rachel   *Daphne du Maurier*